I0758041

THIS ROTTING HEART

SEASONS OF LEGEND

CELESTE BAXENDELL

Copyright © 2025 by Celeste Baxendell

All rights reserved.

No part of this book may be reproduced in any form or by any electronic or mechanical means, including information storage and retrieval systems, without written permission from the author, except for the use of brief quotations in a book review.

No part of this book may be used or reproduced in any form for use in machine learning, large language models, artificial intelligence programs or included in a data set any machine learning, large language models, or artificial intelligence program is trained on.

This is a work of fiction. Names, characters, places, and incidents either are the product of the author's imagination or are used fictitiously. Any resemblance to actual persons, living or dead, events, or locales is entirely coincidental.

CelesteBaxendell.com

Cover Design by Maria Spada

Dust Jacket Illustration by Amira Naval

Interior Design by Celeste Baxendell

 Created with Vellum

To all the girls with hidden hearts

CHAPTER 1

Princess Hellebore stared at the collection of death she'd amassed in front of her, grinning. Her mirth, however, was hidden beneath the goggles over her eyes and the mask over her face, filtering the air she breathed in. She lowered her charcoal as she finished recording her observations of the withering, dying plants.

She didn't envy them. Rotting from the inside out couldn't be pleasant. Although, it wasn't as though Princess Hellebore had ever asked the plants. Not that it mattered. Their only purpose was to suffer.

She looked at her batch of little pots on the end of her table, given the best position in the sunlight in her lab. Well, maybe it wouldn't be so bad for those. Even if they had any awareness—which they didn't—wouldn't it be better to be born with the rot and to never know anything else?

Better that than to be one of the other plants she'd gathered for her experiment, which she had purposefully spread the rot to. They had once known health and would have continued knowing it, if not for their misfortune to have ever encountered Hellebore.

She finished recording the states of all her specimens before tucking her notebook into its assigned pouch on her belt. Then she reached into another pouch and pulled out a labelled vial. With slim metal tweezers and thick leather gloves she went to her first specimen and plucked a few yellow, browning, dry leaves.

She continued on, humming slightly beneath her mask. Its job was to keep any impurities or toxins from getting into her system, but it could not fully shield her from the stench of death. Not that it mattered. She was an alchemist. She'd stopped being bothered by such trivial inconveniences since she'd turned five.

If she hadn't toughened up then, she would have when she'd started attending the Royal Alchemists Academy eight years ago when she'd turned twelve. The Royal Alchemists Academy only took the best, and weak alchemists didn't last long anywhere, much less there. There was no such thing as a squeamish or emotional alchemist.

Once Hellebore had collected her vials for closer observation, she tucked the last vial into her belt and made her way to the door. She could see through the glass someone was already in the other half of the lab, watching Hellebore with sharp eyes. The putrid filth of the slowly dying plants dirtied the glass and made it hard to make anything more out, not that Hellebore needed more than a glimpse to know who it was. The King's Alchemist. Headmistress Palladia.

Or, as Hellebore knew her, Aunt Palladia.

Hellebore stepped into the antechamber where she shut the door firmly behind her. Then she set about pulling her goggles from her head, reaching up and unlatching her mask, taking a full deep breath as she set them on their shelf before she pulled off her thick leather gloves and set them aside as well. Once her hands were free, she lifted them and touched them to the transmutation formula already engraved into the wall and poured her power into it, and the water and soap sitting on the ground glowed. Hellebore closed her eyes as her alchemy went to work, using the materials and cleansing her and her clothes from anything lingering on them. Once the mist faded and she was fresh and new, she opened the second door and stepped out of the antechamber and into the rest of the lab.

Aunt Palladia unfolded her arms and raised an eyebrow. "So?"

Hellebore reached into her belt and pulled out her notebook, passing it over. "See for yourself."

Her aunt took the notebook and started flipping through it as Hellebore pulled a stand closer to the edge of the table and began taking her vials out of their pouches and organizing them. Once Hellebore was satisfied, she grabbed the large magnifying glass that had its own long, arrangeable neck and positioned it so she could examine her first vial in a better light. She touched the formula engraved on the side, tracing it and pushing her power into it, pulling the light coming in from the windows to focus on her vials.

She would never get tired of what alchemy could do.

As Hellebore studied the vein patterns on the leaves in her second vial, her aunt closed the notebook and set it on the table. Aunt Palladia said, "Even after you've turned in your dissertation, here you are still pursuing the project. You're nothing if not dedicated to your project."

Hellebore looked at her through the distorted reflection. "I should hope so. What kind of alchemist would I be if I stopped studying simply because the school year came to a close? But the real question is—"

"You know full well you're going to graduate with honors." Aunt Palladia grinned. "I just spoke with your teachers and got your results. Your hard work has paid off."

"That was a given. That wasn't my question." Hellebore's stomach turned. Was it really her hard work? Or was it because her father was the king and her aunt headmistress?

"Then what is?"

Hellebore swallowed her real question and hid it behind a smirk. "Will they be publishing my results and sending it to the other academies?"

While they might boost her marks in order to ensure her graduation regardless of her merit in order to please her family, surely her teachers wouldn't publish her work if it didn't call for such acclaim, right?

"I haven't yet heard anything about publication, but I have no doubt it will be nominated and in the next rounds, as it deserves," Palladia said, a sharp edge lining her words.

If Palladia took that tone with Hellebore's teachers, then they absolutely would publish her work no matter how undeserving.

Hellebore pulled back, stifling her sigh and ensuring she kept her face impassive as she walked around the table. When she passed the window, she paused and looked out of it. Her lab faced the northeast and with how high up she was, she could see past the walls around the academy and out into the rolling green hills that shifted into rockier craigs, marking the border of Chymes.

The scene was a stark contrast to the rotting plants around her. The vivid green grass and healthy vibrant trees blended with bushes of orange and yellow flowers in full bloom. Even as the terrain shifted into the rockier grounds, flowers and grass could be seen amidst the craigs, brimming with life.

Just beyond it was Iubar. The kingdom of the Sun Elves.

Now a real experiment would be if she could get her hands on one of their famous Sunrise Irises. Being able to see how a magical plant—especially one that was just brimming with the same magic that raced through the Sun Elves' blood—fared against Hellebore's poison and rot would change the game. Using alchemy on a magical plant or creature was a lost art and even in its heyday, something only the best could master. If she could manage it, she'd prove her worth as an alchemist had nothing to do with her blood. And that would only be the beginning. There were so many ways she could use Sunrise Irises.

No living alchemist had ever studied a magical plant or creature. Alchemy, while "magic," was completely different in its structure, unlike the Sunrise Irises or the elves, or even the witches, where magic sang in their blood. Alchemists manipulated, they didn't create. Chymes didn't have magic in its makeup the way Iubar did.

What better way to prove herself worthy to be Palladia's successor than to eclipse her?

The problem? All the Sunrise Irises were on the Sun Elf side of the border.

"Not on your life, Hels." Aunt Palladia's voice brought Hellebore out of her ruminations.

Hellebore shook her head and flashed her aunt a smile, returning to her table. When hadn't Aunt Palladia been able to guess Hellebore's thoughts as they formed?

"I would never. I'm just saying, maybe if things go well, the king of the Sun Elves will soften the terms of our truce and we could politely request an iris. We've been very well behaved for hundreds of years now. I think we've earned a little trust."

Aunt Palladia snorted, crossing her arms as a dark scowl overtook her face, the same one she always wore when the Sun Elves were brought up. "I wouldn't count on it. Those creatures would never give you one simply because you asked nicely. The only way you'd ever be able to get one is to steal one. Or trick an elf into giving you one. While it's been centuries, to them that's nothing. The current king's great-grandfather was the one who lived during the raids and war but for us it's been eight generations."

Hellebore opened her mouth, but Palladia was shaking her head, lifting her hand. "Hels, you have no idea how long their memories are. How long they hold grudges for. Trust me, you'll be lucky if you never lay eyes on one all the days of your life."

"Oh, there's a creature out there who can hold a grudge longer than you?" Hellebore's teasing tone, however, did not banish her aunt's scowl.

"I mean it." Palladia's steely expression cracked for only a brief second. "It's a very good thing you're here at the academy and not in the capital, not that I would have let that happen in the first place. No Sun Elf will get within ten feet of my favorite niece. I'd rather they not get anywhere near your brother, either, but unfortunately your father insisted Callahan be present."

Hellebore rolled her eyes. "That's because if Cal is in meetings with our father and the elves, it means he's not flitting about breaking poor chambermaids' hearts when they see how flaky he is."

Palladia shook her head. "Better a flirtation with a maid than to spend a second with the elves. My brother hasn't told me yet if he's gotten to the bottom of what they're after. I don't believe the elves' excuse for a second that they want to revisit the treaty. They already did when your father took the throne twenty-five years ago."

Hellebore pushed the magnifying glass back to its normal position and began to swap the vials. "The obvious answer is because of the Moon Elves. My former enemy might be a valuable ally against my new one, and all that. Or maybe it involves the upcoming solar eclipse."

Aunt Palladia only pursed her lips, staring out the window and at the border. "Those are the most likely possibilities. It would be foolish of them to come looking for trouble with us, knowing the threat they face from the Moon Elves and the eclipse."

Her aunt's tone, however, betrayed her. Hellebore followed her aunt's gaze. "Did Father tell you why he wanted you to stay here? Meeting with our neighbors and former enemies without the King's Alchemist herself is a strange choice."

Aunt Palladia raised an eyebrow. "Probably because he doesn't want to remind King Taiyo of my existence. Or of alchemists in general. We've met once and that was plenty."

Aunt Palladia's voice scraped over the king's name. Hellebore had never gotten the full story of what happened to make her aunt hate the Sun Elves, especially their king. The times it had come up, her aunt had always waved it away, promising to tell Hellebore when she was older.

And yet, here she was, older, and still no answers.

Hellebore was about to try asking again when her aunt took her by her arm and started leading her out of her lab. "While I, more than anyone, love your dedication, you have been in here for the whole day suffocating on decay, and you need to eat and rest. We'll be leaving for the capital in a week for your graduation, once the elves are gone."

"And?" Hellebore raised an eyebrow as she stepped out into the hallway.

Aunt Palladia wrapped an arm around her and pulled

her into a tight side hug as they walked. "And I'll officially name you as my successor. The next King's Alchemist."

Hellebore squeezed her aunt back, ignoring the hollow feeling in her chest and the voice that whispered she didn't deserve it. Instead, she straightened up and lifted her chin with a proud smirk. "I imagine my father and brother are already fretting about what the two of us will accomplish when I take my position as your successor."

"Your father has been worrying about that since the day you were born. He knew when he laid eyes on you his wife had really just given birth to another me."

"We're just keeping tradition. Every second sibling who proves themselves becomes the King's Alchemist. Really, what's so frightening to him about that?"

"It's not your being an alchemist he's afraid of. It's how much we're alike."

"What's so bad about that?" Hellebore's fingers brushed over her belt. Would she ever be half as skilled as Palladia? "I'm proud to be considered like you in any way. I've always wanted to be. It's my destiny."

Palladia tilted her head. "Well, in every way but one."

Hellebore furrowed her brow, searching her mind for any difference there was between her and her mentor so that she could quickly correct it.

Palladia cleared her throat as they walked through the pristine stone hallways. "Except for the fact that you will marry while that was not my fate."

Oh, right. Hellebore huffed, glancing around to ensure no one was around. "Emerson hasn't said anything about proposing, and neither has Cal. You know how terrible he is with secrets. If my brother's closest friend was thinking of proposing to me after I graduate, wouldn't he tell him? And if Cal knew about it, we would too. He can't keep a secret to save his life."

"The rumor is Emerson will propose after graduation, once he has your father's permission. Why else do you think Emerson went to the capital with your brother? He's asking for your hand, which he should get easily since your father loves anything that would make us less alike."

Hellebore rolled her eyes. "It's not becoming for Headmistresses to be listening to the gossip of idle students."

"Oh, give an aging woman her fun."

They came to a stop, where Hellebore would descend into the lower levels where—if he were at the academy—she would go find Emerson and eat with him in the mess hall as they always did even before they'd entered the flirtation they'd been carrying on for a year now. Well, flirtation on his side. Hellebore tolerated him because he was her brother's oldest friend and a skilled alchemist in his own right. It didn't hurt that he looked good on her arm.

She looked up at her aunt. "Did you ever regret it?"

"Regret what?"

"Not getting married, having children?"

Palladia turned to face Hellebore, putting her hands on her shoulders before reaching up and cupping her cheeks. "Never. Not since the day I held your brother and then four years later you as well. What need do I have for children when I have loved you as my own since your birth and your mother's passing?"

"You never desired a marriage of your own?"

Palladia sighed. "It was not the path for me. And while we might be alike, that is where we will differ, because I know it is meant for you."

Hellebore nodded, biting her tongue. She wasn't convinced it was. But Emerson was acceptable, he was an alchemist, from a good family, and a loyal friend to her brother. If Hellebore had never been born, he would be the obvious choice to be the next King's Alchemist. Hellebore and Emerson were a perfect match on paper. But what if she was like Palladia and she wasn't meant for it?

Would he be miserable? Would she?

Would they all be better off if she kept to the exact path her aunt walked? Was she even worthy of that path? How could she really know if she deserved everything that had been given to her?

Hellebore looked at the window again and the craigs in the distance.

What she did know was that she wasn't going to be on the border and so close to a Sunrise Iris for long.

No one ever needed to know.

CHAPTER 2

Hellebore was scaling down the outer wall of the academy grounds when the sound of the guards' voices caused her to freeze in place, feet braced against the wall. But none of the voices were near her.

She looked to the side and out into the night to see two riders approaching the academy's walls at a furious, breakneck pace. Wait... She recognized those horses.

Callahan and Emerson. What were they doing racing back to the academy when she and Aunt Palladia were about to travel to the capital?

She'd find out as soon as she got back with her treasure. If the Sun Elves would never give them a Sunrise Iris, she'd just sneak one away and they'd never notice. They were scheduled to be back in Iubar by the time she and Palladia reached the capital.

She'd never show anyone. But she needed it. If she had it and managed feats in secret no other living alchemist could, she could rest assured she did deserve her position.

She waited for the gates to open and her brother and Emerson to race through before she finished her descent.

She hit the ground and transmuted her thin rope back into the coat it had originally been and then she shrugged it on over her blouse, kirtle, and skirt, bustled up into her belt. She then slunk into the shadows, kept low to the ground, and hurried off to the border.

Hellebore knew she wouldn't have long, not with Emerson and Callahan's return, but if she'd gone back, she wouldn't get another chance. So she ran as fast as she could once she was out of the guards' sight, her braid whipping through the air and her belt full of tools painfully jostling against her waist and hips.

Dawn was breaking as she reached the rocky craigs that marked the border, and she immediately started clambering down the slopes and deeper into enemy territory. Once she was on the other side, she paused, taking the time to catch her breath and to start looking around for any irises.

But there were no plants. Not... too odd, given the rocky soil. She would have to go deeper. She forced herself to press on, climbing up over rocks, seeing a large forest in the distance grow larger as she got closer. That was farther beyond the border than she wanted to go, but she would have to if this stretch wasn't producing—

Hellebore stopped as she spotted a few flowers springing up between rocks. Unfortunately, they weren't Sunrise Irises. It was hard to tell what they were, even as she knelt on the ground in front of them. She flipped open her notebook to her sketch of the flowers in her current experiments and held it up to the drooping, brittle, browning thing.

They were different species but the same appearance. It was sick. Strange.

If she had an extra pot, she would have taken one.

Instead, she pushed herself to her feet and pressed on.

She was crossing the last stretch of boulders before an empty field that led up to the forest when she finally spotted the brilliant, glowing orange, gold, and pink iris that she was looking for. She reached into a pouch and checked her Alchemist's Compass, pointing right at the flower in front of her.

A Sunrise Iris.

An Alchemist's Compass pointed in the direction of whatever the formula written on its back determined. Hellebore had hers set to point in the direction of Sun Elf magic, the same type the Sunrise Iris had.

Hellebore knelt in front of it, dropping her compass to the ground beside her. She pulled out her pot and trowel from their respective pockets and began to carefully prepare the pot and dig up the plant without killing it. The formulas etched into her gloves helped as she was able to pour her power into them and activate the formulas as needed to repair any damage to the plant that occurred. The sun had fully risen by the time she got the flower safely into the pot and she started packing up, but then she looked over to see her compass's needle spinning wildly.

A shadow blocked the warm sun on her back.

Her stomach dropped.

She looked up. At first glance, he looked like a human man, especially as the sun behind him made it harder to make out his features. However, he tilted his head as he looked down at her. The sunlight highlighted the sloping point of his ear and showed that while half of his hair was black, it shifted into orange and gold farther down, perfectly matching the potted iris sitting in her lap.

Her compass had settled on pointing directly at him.

A Sun Elf.

Her Iubian Elvish was rusty, but she managed a, "Hello..."

She'd been caught iris-handed.

And as she looked around, this wasn't a random elf who'd wandered near the border as well. There were several more scattered around them as well, and given their manner of dress, she'd bet they were a patrol. They were likely there specifically to catch any greedy little alchemists who got in over their heads trying to steal flowers, or worse, elves for experiments.

The one standing over her turned to the others and said something so quickly Hellebore wasn't able to make out any of it before he started to bend down to grab her arm. They were going to arrest her. Which, if she was being fair, they had every right to.

Her father was going to be *furious*.

And they would have a hostage. At least if she could get back over the border, her only problem would be her father's wrath.

Hellebore hadn't come into enemy territory unprepared. She grabbed her trowel and swung with all her strength, slamming it into the elf's leg. He stumbled, letting out a muffled grunt as he lost his balance, and she shot to her feet. She started running, but there were six other Sun Elves she had to get past.

She reached into a pouch and quickly activated the formula, throwing the pellets as she did so. Smoke poured out, flooding the area. She considered for a second trying to take the iris with her, but thought better of it, abandoning it and focusing on preserving her life and country's dignity. She pulled her mask out of her bag and held it to her face as she started running while the air filled with coughs.

A voice ripped through the air, shouting the same word again and again between coughs.

Hellebore at least hoped to make it to the rockier part of the stretch where she might be able to hide long enough for them to think they lost her. She had no hope of actually outrunning elves.

A hand grabbed her arm as she tried to duck past one of them, and it ripped the mask from her face. She quickly turned, used her other hand to reach into another pouch, pulling out her knife and slicing the arm of whoever had grabbed her. The second the elf started bleeding, Hellebore took advantage of it.

It was do or die.

She'd already violated the treaty trying to take the iris; how much worse could it be to use a little blood if it would get her to safety?

She took the knife and cut into her glove, altering the formula as she took hold of the magic in the blood and began transmuting. She ripped the sun magic out of the elf's blood and made it hers to command, sending a blade of light in a circle around her, knocking the elves back.

Any other day she would have been basking in such a historic achievement.

There'd be time for that later. She released the elf and took off again, but without her mask, she was coughing horribly. She only made it a few steps before a weight slammed into her back and she went crashing to the ground. The smoke began to clear as the weight pressed down harder and hands grabbed hers, pulling them up above her head and far away from her belt and curling around them to trap her fingers so she couldn't do any alchemy.

She looked up out of the corner of her eye to see it was the original elf pinning her down, but he didn't look satisfied. He was panting for breath and glaring at her.

One of the other elves spoke and Hellebore thought the sentence translated to something about "having her" and "want to do now."

He stared down at her, her face turned and one side pressed into the dirt. She narrowed her eyes right back at him.

He muttered something. He might have said something about "doing things the hard way," but she was too dazed to be sure.

Then he looked up at the elf who had spoken and said something involving "difficult," "run," and "restrain."

Then he released her hands, quickly shifting to her waist, and she gasped when her belt loosened and he pulled it back, passing it to another elf. She tried to get her arms under her and crawl out from under him, but his weight on her back kept her pinned as he grabbed her arms and pulled them behind her back.

He ripped her gloves off her hands, cursing at the blood still on them.

She closed her eyes as he staggered to his feet while another elf began binding her wrists together. If the Sun Elves didn't kill her, her father was going to.

Maybe she should let the Sun Elves do whatever they liked to do with alchemists. It couldn't be pleasant, but maybe it was better than having to face her father and the consequences of her foolishness.

CHAPTER 3

While Hellebore was a princess, as an alchemist, she was not squeamish or priggish, but having her hands bound behind her and being thrown over the shoulder of the elf who had caught her was the most undignified situation she'd been in.

She faced his back, his arm wrapped around her legs, holding her in place as his shoulder dug into her stomach. She would have preferred being dragged through the dirt to this. Honestly, for all they knew she was a random alchemist, so why not give her a few bumps and bruises while transporting her?

While the heat flooding her whole body at the humiliating position refused to ebb, she instead tried to focus on what she did remember about Iubian Elvish. Unfortunately, they'd mostly fallen silent as she hung over his back, blood rushing to her head.

She glanced at her alchemist's belt in the other hand of the elf carrying her. Her hands were bound, but if she could twist just enough, the pouch closest to her—

She let out a sharp yelp when she was jostled and the

hand gripping her legs tightened. And then the elf spoke in her language, "Stop it. You've been enough trouble, alchemist."

He spat the word alchemist like it was an insult and not a badge of honor. Reluctantly, she understood why she was the monster in his eyes.

Finally, she was no longer upside down but was being thrown into a carriage and went rear over front until she came to a stop in a jumbled heap on the floor of it, hands still bound. She rolled over onto her front to see her captor moving to shut the door, back to speaking Iubian Elvish as he directed the elf carrying the Sunrise Iris and another approached him with reins to a horse.

"You speak Chymesian?" Hellebore called out.

He turned back and raised an eyebrow. "Enough. The way you speak enough Iubian Elvish."

Hellebore wouldn't personally qualify what she spoke as enough, given she'd been unable to translate most of what she'd heard. Why he thought she could was beyond her, but before she could respond, he shut the door.

Within seconds, the carriage was rolling forward, taking out the legs Hellebore had managed to get under her and sending her to the floor again with a loud thud. She heard a laugh on the other side.

Her cheeks burned furiously as she got back up, awkwardly with her hands behind her, to take a more dignified seat on the bench.

Alright. She was a captive, in a carriage, and—she peered out the window—heading deeper into Iubian territory. Now she needed to decide if she was going to let them think she was a random, rogue alchemist to try to escape, or accept whatever trial and punishment that awaited her for trying to take a Sunrise Iris and using a Sun Elf's blood in her attempted escape, or tell them exactly who she was and hope that afforded her protection without costing Chymes too much.

Her racing heart refused to slow, and Hellebore had to close her eyes and take long, deep breaths. She could not panic. She would not lose her head. If she was going to get through this with the least amount of damage possible, she needed to remove all distracting emotions and feel absolutely nothing. It was the only way to think clearly.

She kept watching out the window, observing the patrol that captured her.

Why had a border patrol had a carriage to throw her into in the first place? Right, their king was still in Chymes. Maybe they'd been assigned to wait for his party at the border to swap out for a fresh carriage? But then why would they use it for her?

Unless of course the king had already passed through and taken the fresh carriage, leaving behind the tired horses, which would then be her carriage. Callahan and Emerson would only have been able to arrive if the talks were over and everything settled.

Hellebore wrestled with her twisting heart; this wasn't the time to miss her brother. She needed to think of him with only cold reason attached.

So if everything had been settled between Chymes and Iubar, that was a point in favor of revealing her identity. They couldn't change any terms in order to negotiate her safety without having to reenter negotiations entirely, and if she apologized to the king and explained she was a great admirer of plants—she wasn't, only in the way they died— maybe he'd be forgiving.

She looked at the elf she'd cut open, who was brushing a hand over the bandage wrapped around her arm. Maybe not, since she'd cut open one of his border guards and used her blood for an alchemic attack against them.

If trying to steal the plant was a crime punishable by death, stealing their blood ensured an agonizing execution. Even if they didn't kill her, they would want Chymes to pay dearly.

No. After trying to fight her way out, her best chance was still a brilliant escape, if she could manage one. She couldn't trust a Sun Elf to have mercy on her even if he knew she was a princess.

The voice in her head saying that sounded exactly like Aunt Palladia.

Nightfall would be her best chance. It was when the Sun Elves were the weakest. During the Great Abductions, the alchemists had always succeeded because they'd raided the elves at night.

The Great Abductions were an atrocity of her people's from over five hundred years ago where they'd stolen Sun Elves and used their blood to access their magic in their alchemy, creating weapons, tools, and anything their imaginations and formulas could transmute the magic into. Her people had paid dearly for it. The Sun Elves had spilled her people's blood above and beyond what the alchemists had spilled in their studies. The conflicts leading to the raids and the ensuing war of that age had been deep and complicated, and none of it changed the fact that Hellebore was going to use the elves' biological and magical disadvantage under the moon to her advantage.

She certainly wasn't going to try and abscond with an elf to experiment on. She wasn't even going to try and take the iris—unless, of course an opportunity presented itself.

In the meantime, she acted like she was watching the scenery, but instead strained her ears for any conversation around her so that she could brush the rust off her Iubian Elvish and understand what was going on. Callahan had always been the one better at foreign languages and politics; he had no choice in the matter. Hellebore had protested at the lessons since she was destined to go to the Royal Alchemist's Academy and become the King's Alchemist. She regretted that flippant attitude now but was grateful that despite her flippant attitude, she had gotten good marks on her assignments, so there had to be some knowledge of Iubian still in her head.

The elf who had captured her rode toward the front, occasionally looking back at her with narrowed eyes. He didn't speak much to anyone. However, he had an air about him and from the way the other elves treated him, she assumed he had to be the captain of the patrol.

The two closest to her had a quiet conversation, giving Hellebore the opportunity to brush off her translation skills. The male elf nodded at the female's bandaged arm and asked, "Are you alright?"

The female nodded. "I will be."

He said something Hellebore couldn't quite make out except for the end. "—alchemist. Any opportunity to take our blood, they take. Savages."

The female clucked her tongue and fixed him with a stern look, but her tone betrayed her frustration with herself. "I should have been more careful not to let—wishful thinking on his part—cold feet—not come willingly."

It was like dusting off an old shelf. Hellebore's Iubian Elvish was coming back to her and as long as she could hear clearly and they didn't speak too quickly, she could understand the gist.

The male shot a glare at Hellebore, who was staring up at the clouds with a perfectly practiced bored expression, and muttered, "—not natural."

"She's a human alchemist. She's not concerned with natural."

They fell into silence, and Hellebore watched the sun travel through the sky. She shifted her shoulders, focusing on the feeling of the rope against her wrists. The elves had good reason to fear the alchemists. There was little they couldn't do as long as they had the right material and the right formula. A skilled alchemist could create a formula to accomplish their means on the fly. Hellebore's current problem was she had no way to write the formula she needed to transmute the rope from its solid, bound form to a thinner, more fragile form she could escape from.

So when the sun finished setting and the carriage came to a stop, Hellebore had made no progress in getting the ropes off. But the door to the carriage opened and it was the captain from before. He held open the door and gestured for her to come out with one hand, holding her belt in the other.

He said in Chymesian, "Come here, alchemist."

She bristled at being given so clear an order, but she did as he said. It wasn't ideal, but even formulas written in dirt still worked.

They were deep in the forest now, and the elves around her were quickly setting up camp for the night. As soon as she reached the edge, the captain took her arm and helped her down, not letting go as he led her over to one of the fires. She couldn't see him quite as well in the darkening night, but as they reached the fire, it bathed his cool, amber-hued skin in a warm golden light. He let go, and she stumbled to the ground. He stood above her and raised an eyebrow. "Will you cooperate?"

She replied in Iubian, a thick accent over her words, "Will you give chance?"

His cold, hard expression shifted. He stepped back and nodded.

She spoke slowly, stumbling over the foreign language,

"You cannot—Crossing the border is not crime. Iris did not leave Iubar."

She had to at least try the defense.

He stared at her. Then he laughed. He wrapped an arm around his stomach as he stepped back. The other elves stared at them for a moment, like he was growing a second head instead of laughing at her argument.

He lowered himself to the ground, chuckling even as she glared at him. "Princess Hellebore, you are brave, like they said. However, you are foolish if you think you are getting out of this."

So they knew who she was. Which meant she *needed* to escape. She watched the other elves out of the corner of her eye. Most of them were eating their rations or going to their tents, yawning and visibly ragged now that the sun had vanished. She lifted her chin. "This is a mis—misunderstanding."

"I caught you stealing a Sunrise Iris." His voice turned icy cold, cutting through the heat of the fire beside them. "You knew exactly what you were doing. Do not lie to me."

"So..." Hellebore paused, searching for the words, her thick accent slowing her down. "The treaty talk... not well?"

Was she a valuable hostage? Were they at war? Or was she just an impetuous princess who took a flower she was suspecting meant more to the Sun Elves than anyone in Chymes knew?

If the former, that could have been what Callahan and Emerson had been riding to the academy for.

And like a fool she'd just given herself over. Even if her father would be reluctant to compromise for her return, Callahan and Aunt Palladia would never let him leave her with the elves.

The captain snorted. "Do not test me, alchemist."

There was something Hellebore was missing. But if

playing along would be better for her escape, she'd take the confusion then.

She bowed her head for a moment and then said, "Apologies."

He blinked, and then he shifted, taking her by the shoulder and turning her around and releasing her hands from the rope. What a fool.

She kept her face impassive as he returned to her front and offered her a waterskin. She rubbed her red, raw wrists and eyed it. He sighed, uncorked it, and took a sip. He held it out again and said, "What would I accomplish by poisoning you?"

A fair assertion if she was his hostage; she would have no value to him if she was dead. She slowly took it, placing her other hand on the ground behind her, in her shadow. The captain's eyes never left her face as she lifted it to her lips. She took a sip as her fingers started drawing in her formula in the dirt. She held it back out to him as she finished her formula and pushed her power into it.

He took it, but didn't drink. He just recorked it and set it on the ground next to her belt, fixing her with a stern look. "What did you hope to—"

His last few words she couldn't quite make out. She blinked at him for a moment. He sighed and switched to Chymesian. "What did you hope to accomplish with your reckless actions?"

"I'm just a simple human princess utterly enamored with pretty flowers." She looked up at him through her eyelashes, trying to look as empty-headed and harmless as the most famous damsels in legend. "Please don't hold my nature against me."

He scowled. "Your false innocence is as sheer as gauze."

"I have no idea what you're referring to."

He sighed. "If you will cooperate and accept this, everything will be much easier for you. I wish you no ill. That's not why you're here."

Had they come looking for her specifically to take her as a hostage and not simply gotten lucky because of her foolishness? Had they been coming to kidnap her from the academy, and Callahan and Emerson had been hurrying to come protect her? But...

"Why? As in, why me? What are you hoping to get out of this?"

His eyes widened and then he shifted back. "What more would I need than to secure peace between our people?"

He was hiding something. But then he picked up the waterskin and she no longer cared about his secrets. He took a sip before setting it to the side and picking up her belt. It took all of Hellebore's willpower to maintain her façade and bury the grin trying to crawl onto her face. She couldn't give it away. She just had to be patient. He started fiddling with the pouches despite her glaring at him. "You carry quite a... an arsenal, you might call it?"

"I am an alchemist. Does that surprise you?"

"But no supplies? How far did you expect to get?"

His Chymesian was about as good as her Iubian was, given she had no clue what he was trying to get at.

"Look, all I wanted was the iris. If I'd known it would be this big of a deal, I wouldn't have gone after it. I thought it was just a flower that you all have plenty of. I wasn't trying to run off with an elf."

"Yet, I am running off with you." His lips twitched up, but his eyes were starting to flutter as her sedative kicked in. He blinked, trying to focus his gaze on her. "What concerns me is how you used my injured guard to steal our magic even though such practices are long forgotten by your people in the name of peace. If any alchemist can cut an elf and use us—"

"I'm not just any alchemist, and I was simply trying to get away. I made an educated guess about the required modifications to a formula already on my glove that would assist me in escaping, and I was correct. I wasn't trying to turn her into an experiment."

"You are Palladia's..." His voice dropped to a murmur, trailing off into a cough.

Did he know her aunt personally? Or just by reputation?

He tried to clear his throat and then opened one of the pouches to reveal nothing inside. His brow furrowed, and he started to look at her. She couldn't hold back her grin anymore as he slumped over while the sedative took control.

She whispered, "Sweet dreams."

A shout went up from one of the elves on guard duty, but Hellebore had already ripped her belt out of his hands. "I'll be taking this with me, thank you!"

She slung it on as she reached into another pouch when a hand encircled her ankle. She looked down to see the captain's face screwed up. He was choking on his breath while trying to keep her in place.

She froze.

What she'd transmuted into the water from her belt was meant to put him to a peaceful sleep. It wasn't supposed to cause any damage. He was choking and gasping, and it was clear as his face turned red this was not something he would likely survive.

She could easily rip her ankle out of his weakening grip, but...

She might not want to be a hostage, but killing a Sun Elf in her escape wasn't going to do her people any favors. The elves were shouting, but she dropped to the ground and quickly wrote a new formula in the dirt and pushed her power into it. She put her other hand over the captain and began separating the sedative in him from the water in his stomach. Once she had the sedative completely separated, she pushed it up and drew it out.

He jolted, turning on his side and with a wretched noise, he emptied himself of the apparently fatal sedative.

His breathing cleared right as two elves grabbed her by her arms and hauled her up, ripping her through the air and away from the captain.

The captain lay on the ground as another elf rushed up to his side, possibly a healer, but the captain's gaze was on Hellebore as she was dragged away until his eyes fluttered shut. Her arms were bound behind her again, her chance of escape gone, and she was thrown back into the carriage.

As she lay on her back, bruises forming on her shoulders and legs from the way she'd been thrown in, and from one of the guards being extremely rough with her, she stared at the ceiling.

She should have let him die.

CHAPTER 4

The next day their party grew larger—at least Hellebore heard more horses and another set of wheels, but she was only let out of the carriage for basic necessities. Afterwards, her hands were rebound and she was roughly shoved back in.

She didn't see the captain again. Her collection of bruises changed day by day. Had what she'd done even worked or had she failed to save the elf from her unintended homicide? If it hadn't, she'd sacrificed her chance to escape for nothing because now they had her on murder *and* practicing alchemy on an elf. Plus, stealing a magical plant and using the blood of an elf for transmutation. Her status as a princess might go a long way protecting her from physical harm, but those offenses stacked together and not even her status would save her from execution.

Finally, when she was brought out of the carriage after two weeks of traveling, it wasn't to a forest surrounding them. Well, mostly. There were still lush trees and sunlight streaming in over the leaves, but there was also a wall. She looked over her shoulder as her guards put her on her feet

to see a massive castle stretching up into the sky, framed by the mountains around them. They were in the capital, Auror.

She was being pushed forward, unable to really look around as elves rushed about. A female elf came striding out of the castle, a baby elfling on her hip. Given the circlet on her head, Hellebore imagined this had to be some relation of the king. The pattern on her dress was familiar, but when Hellebore looked around, she didn't spy it on any of the elves she'd traveled with. Where had she seen it then?

Then she was being shoved through the doors and hauled through hallways, no one bothering to say a word to her about where she was being taken. Was she going to meet the king and would he reveal what he was going to do with her? Or why he had been apparently targeting her in the first place?

But instead of being taken down, they went up. She wasn't being held in the dungeons, at least. She tried out her Iubian again. "Where are we going?"

The two elves looked at each other, and the one on the right shook his head. The one on her left said, "Your room."

"And the king?"

That earned her harsh glares from both of them. "The king will see you when he desires, alchemist."

Then they were in front of a door, and once more she was being pushed inside somewhere. They didn't remove the rope binding her wrists, which was driving her insane with the way it had rubbed her skin raw and broken it so it bled. They just shut the door and locked it.

They'd had the foresight not to give her her belt back. Not that there was much she could do now. If she'd failed to escape the little patrol that had caught her in the forest, she knew she wasn't going to make it out of the castle and the city without being caught. With the mountains around them and the terrain outside the city she'd observed, there was probably only one main road out, if she even made it that far.

Hellebore still took stock of the room just to see if there was anything useful in it.

Huh. The room was nice, far nicer than she anticipated even as a royal hostage. It was the height of luxury, or... if this wasn't the height of luxury for Sun Elves, she couldn't imagine what that *did* look like. There was a four poster, gilded, canopy bed covered in plush pink and orange blankets. On the other side of the room was a tall dresser made of the same soft white wood as the bed and a vanity with a gold framed mirror, and next to it, a deep wardrobe that matched, with gold trim in swirling sun and iris patterns. Toward the front of the room was a sitting area with a low table, a sofa, and a few plush chairs, all trimmed in the same bright, sunny colors—orange, gold, pink. On the table was a vase of flowers in the same colors, though unfortunately no Sunrise Irises. Just normal, but pretty, flowers.

Why were there fresh flowers? Did they put fresh flowers in every room? Or...

Hellebore turned on her heels, looking up at the ceiling, a stunning painting of a sunrise splashing the surface in gold, orange, and pink.

Had they been expecting her?

She made her way over to the window and peered out into the courtyard, using her sore, bruised shoulder to nudge the shimmering gold curtain out of the way.

The activity had slowed. The royal—whether she'd been the queen or a princess, Hellebore wasn't sure—was gone. As far as she knew, King Taiyo wasn't married, but knowledge of minutiae like that wasn't her area. Their neighbors and the politics of foreign affairs were all Callahan's arena.

She desperately wished Callahan was with her, and not for politics. If he were there, she would be able to trust nothing bad could happen to her. Callahan wouldn't let it.

But he wasn't. So, missing the way her brother always crushed her to him every time she'd returned home from the academy didn't do her any good.

The last of the patrol was being cleared away. Hellebore moved farther down the room to the next window—her room was obscenely large—and did the same, catching sight of the next courtyard over, connected to the first but separate enough. She spotted bushes of orange, gold, and pink flowers, the ones that made up the bouquet on her table. But what was most interesting were the servants scurrying about it, seemingly deep in some kind of preparation. Some court event maybe taking place there?

A banquet for the king who had returned shortly before they received their human hostage?

Hellebore sighed, trying to roll out the stiffness and the ache in her shoulders, but not being able to do much with her hands still bound. After a few hours of trying to rest while shifting from spot to spot to find something comfortable, she gave up. Instead, she did another lap around the room, looking at everything around her and coming up with a dozen ways she could use her alchemy on them to fashion tools for escape or weapons to protect herself, but knowing it was all fantasy.

With some awkward, slow positioning and work, she opened the drawers of the dresser to see it was full of clothes in the Sun Elf style, lots of shiny, spotless silks that were completely impractical in her mind. As she stared at the dresses in the wardrobe, all she could think of was how the hems were so long they'd trail behind her and the nice fabrics would be ruined in a lab. The harsh cleaning treatment the alchemists used when purifying themselves while around toxic substances would render the delicate fabrics to shreds.

Whose room was this? They couldn't have been expecting her for long, and all of these clothes clearly indicated this room was lived in.

Her stomach sank. Unless the king had been planning on kidnapping her before he'd ever even left for Chymes. Hellebore wasn't a fan of those implications, so she pushed the ludicrous idea away. Why would the king go through the elaborate ruse of visiting her father in the name of peace just to steal her away? He could have taken a page out of the alchemists' book and just raided the academy to steal her. But that didn't even explain what he would want with her.

No. While possible, it certainly wasn't plausible. Her fear was simply getting the better of her, and if she had a knife and the right formula, she would have cut it out of her. Since she could not, she just pushed it away. Logic dictated the most reasonable explanation was that she was in someone else's room, and that female elf had simply been displaced for the time being.

Hellebore then made her way over to the wall closest to the bed and tried the second door there, but it was locked. And the sun was setting.

And clearly, she wasn't going to be fed, so at least that was consistent with her hostage expectations even if inconvenient.

The next morning, she woke up when her door flew open and she startled, knocking one of the pillows to the ground as two female elves came into the room while two hovered at the door. The two guards who entered were dressed in matching uniforms, likely servants, while the other two at the door were clearly guards. At the sight of her, completely disheveled and dirtying the pristine bed, one of the servants gasped.

The other tutted under her breath and said, "The king will not be happy about this."

Well, if the king cared that much, he could have come and seen her for himself and at least given her the use of her hands back. Although he was smart not to. She was deadly when all she needed was her hands and something to write with in order to bend the world to her will.

"Come, Your Highness, we must clean you up," the first one said, hurrying to her side.

Hellebore snapped, "Your king doesn't want his hostage to look like one?"

At their blank stares, she realized she'd spoken in Chymesian and repeated herself in Iubian, her words losing some of their bite as she had to walk slowly through the words. But even when using their tongue, they didn't respond.

She didn't know if they couldn't understand her beneath her accent or if they simply chose to ignore her comment. Likely the second.

Instead, the servants helped her to her feet and undid her hands. The first maid gasped at Hellebore's bleeding wrists before shooting a glare at the guard. One of the guards shrugged. "She's an alchemist."

The next second, a tub was being carried into the room by another set of female servants, who began filling it with water and using their magic to heat it. Hellebore watched them intently, taking a little pleasure in how the longer her gaze stayed on them, the more their hands shook. The original two servants exchanged glances as they pulled fresh clothes from the wardrobe. One of the guards at the door took a few steps toward Hellebore, moving to stand between her and the elves using magic.

Before Hellebore could speak, one of the original elves grabbed the guard by the arm and hissed, "Stop that. You know His Majesty's orders. She's not doing any harm."

Hellebore turned her head slightly, catching the guard's eyes and grinning.

The guard ripped her arm out of the servant's grip. "Maybe not yet, she's not, but you see that look in her eyes. She's—them all with her eyes, and if she had a knife, she'd be doing even worse."

She'd missed one word, but overall she wasn't doing too poorly.

Hellebore turned her head to face the guard fully and lied through her smile. "Actually, I'm focusing on translating your language in my mind. Forgive me, my Iubian is rough."

The guard returned to her post, hand on the hilt of her sword, eyes tracking Hellebore's every move. The second servant cleared her throat and cut in, pulling Hellebore to her feet.

Then the original two elves were trying to help Hellebore out of her dirty clothes, but the construction was clearly foreign to them, and Hellebore shoved them off. "I am capable of getting out of my clothes myself. I am a princess, but I have lived most of my life without—" The word for attendants escaped her, so she fumbled for another one. "—without maids."

When she was a student at the academy, she lived like all the other students, no servants or special treatment.

At least, that's the way it was supposed to be. She hadn't had the servants, but she was never sure about the special treatment.

When Hellebore had returned to the castle for holidays and breaks, it had always been a strange adjustment for her to get used to being attended by servants, specifically disrobing and bathing in front of strangers. However, she figured this was on the lower end of uncomfortable things about being a hostage, and there were far worse, so she'd accept this strange situation. At least the guards were female.

Of course she caught the whispers of the girls, but she couldn't blame them too much. She was a foreign species to them, and she was rather bruised from the rough handling, not to mention the scars she'd accumulated from experiments gone wrong.

She ignored them and safely sank into the tub, hissing when her raw, cracked wrists hit the warm water. The stinging sensation went right up into her jaw, but the heat did help relax her sore back and ease the ache in her shoulders.

"Your Highness, your wrists, let us—"

She held up her vivid red wrist and snapped, "Unless it's an order from your king, don't. If he wants a cleaned-up hostage, I will oblige, but do not push me further."

She remembered the word for oblige; that was a victory.

The servant fell silent and simply returned to waiting off to the side with a towel. Hellebore gritted her teeth and ignored the stinging in her wrists with every motion as she cleaned herself from head to toe. While she did so, some of the maidens stripped the dirty bedding and replaced it with a matching fresh set. Hellebore ran her fingers through her warm, brown hair.

She stepped out of the tub only for the servants to attempt once more to take over, and this time she let them as they dried her off and got her into a shift that was a foreign style, but it was at least some covering. That was when three more female elves came in with an assortment of tools and fabrics and the measuring tapes around their shoulders that left Hellebore assuming they were seamstresses. The two guards rolled their eyes; one crossed her arms and muttered something that Hellebore thought translated to something involving "commotion" and the "lifespan of a fly." One of the servants stifled a laugh at whatever the guard said, both receiving glares from the original pair of maids.

The three seamstresses moved in a whirlwind, having Hellebore lift her arms and positioning her to their liking as they took a flurry of measurements and held up fabrics to her face, all talking so fast Hellebore caught very little of it. What she did catch was about fabrics and necklines and a comment about wide hips Hellebore should probably be offended by. Her cheeks flushed, but she managed to stay still and hold her tongue.

Now she knew what her experiments must have felt like being measured, poked and prodded all the time.

It was humbling if nothing else.

Were her hips really that wide?

If they were going to eye her hips and legs with such disdain, they could give her back her Chymesian clothes and just let her be the filthy savage they all thought she was. But before she could pitch the idea, the seamstresses were done and gone.

Then the maids threw a dress from the wardrobe over her head. Hellebore let them since the style was different than her usual skirts and blouses and she wouldn't know where to begin to secure it.

Once she was dressed, she looked around to see the other servants were gone, and she was left with just the guards and the original pair of maids. They sat her in front of the vanity and handled her hair.

The two bickered about a style for a minute before Hellebore said, "Does it really matter? Just—" As her mind blanked on the Iubian word for braid, she made the motion with her fingers. "—then pin it."

"Do you mean braid?" the taller of the two asked.

Hellebore snapped her fingers and pointed at her. "Yes. That. Braid it."

The girls obeyed, quickly doing two braids and wrapping them around her head in a crown, pinning it into place.

Finally, they seemed to be done, and when she rose from her seat to be escorted to the king who apparently was fussier about her appearance than she was, the shorter maiden shook her head and said, "No, His Majesty will come see you later."

Hellebore huffed and moved to sit on the sofa where a breakfast tray sat as they left. The guards stayed, perfectly silent. Smart. The guards were staying inside the room to make sure now that Hellebore had her hands, she didn't try anything.

The sun kept climbing into the sky, and when it reached its apex, the door finally opened. She'd been staring at her injured wrists, ignoring the guards, and looked up to see the captain from before in her doorway.

So he wasn't dead. That was a relief. She didn't need to see the king with murder as one of the charges against her.

If she was a hostage, she needed to be a sympathetic one.

He looked much better than the last time she'd seen him. She rose from her seat, and his quick stride halted when she did. He looked up from the door and froze at the sight of her.

She raised an eyebrow as his eyes skimmed over her, looking like a Sun Elf and far less like a mad alchemist. His eyes darted back up to her face, and his expression steeled as he finished stepping into the room. He gave the female guards a nod, and they departed, shutting the door behind them.

Wait...

She spoke in Iubian. "What is going on?"

He paused in front of the door. "What?"

"The maids—they said the king was going to come see me."

He stared at her. As the moment stretched down, a sinking feeling settled over her, especially as she looked him over, studying the pattern he was wearing. It was the same as the royal she'd seen the day before.

Oh no.

She'd thought the hole she'd dug for herself couldn't get deeper. She had been very wrong.

CHAPTER 5

Hellebore stared at the Sun Elf in front of her.

King Taiyo.

This whole time...

He'd been King Taiyo since the moment he'd stood over her, catching her with the iris, and had still been King Taiyo when she'd nearly killed him trying to sedate him.

It'd been nice living while she'd had the chance.

Finally, he took a step toward her, speaking slowly, his melodic voice rumbling over the words. "I am the king."

There was no point pretending to be agreeable now. She'd almost killed the king and there was no doubt that armies were being drafted to go back into the centuries-dead war she'd just resurrected.

So Hellebore had no qualms shooting out of her seat and hissing, "And you waited until *now* to tell me?"

Taiyo's hand cut through the air as he gestured, voice sharpening, a slight laugh in his tone. "Who did you think I was? Who else would I be?"

"I don't know! I thought you were arresting me for

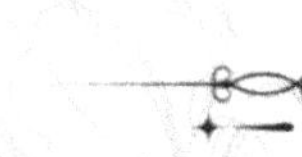

stealing the iris. But now—" She switched back to Chymesian as her mind was spinning faster than her Iubian Elvish could keep up. "Now I'm utterly lost. Whose room is this?" She grabbed the skirts of the dress she wore as she advanced on him. "Whose clothes are these? Why am I here? What do you want with me?"

King Taiyo took a long, deep breath, closed his eyes, and she couldn't quite tell whether his pained expression was anger at her, frustration, or something else.

He also switched to Chymesian when he opened his eyes. His voice came out from his gritted teeth. "You're not playing dumb. You don't know."

If Hellebore hadn't already almost killed him, she would have been severely tempted to strangle him right then. Her voice came out much harsher than his. "*What* am I supposed to know? Am I not being held as a hostage against my father?"

King Taiyo let out a laugh, but it was bitter and hollow. "This room is your room. Those clothes are yours. The preparations going on outside? They're for our wedding."

He meant war. Surely, he meant they were preparing for *war*.

"Our wedding?" Hellebore stepped forward, narrowing her eyes, but not even her years trying to divest herself of worthless emotions like hysteria could stop her voice from pitching up as her breathing shallowed. She kept moving, unable to stop now. "You can't—you must be using the wrong word. Wedding—*that* word means a ceremony in which we would become husband and wife."

He took another step closer, arm extended and palm facing her, but she was pacing too quickly for it to matter. His voice steadied, chasing her around the room. "I know what I said. We are betrothed. Your father approved of the match and claimed he sent word to you and you accepted."

She pressed her palm against her stomach, but it did nothing to help her catch her breath. It was her turn to laugh, dangerously high and shallow. "And if that was true, what did you think I was doing digging up one of your irises? If you thought I'd agreed, why have you been treating me like a prisoner?"

"Let me explain." Taiyo took a few steps, trying to follow her, but she just whipped around each time, putting more distance between them, her skirts whirling. "When I arrived at the academy and discovered you weren't there, I thought it was simply a matter of cold feet, as you humans put it. I went after you in order to speak some reason into you and give you assurances about our match. Then, I caught you stealing an iris and you attacked me. Twice. It didn't occur to me you didn't know of our engagement when I'd been assured you did. I thought you'd feigned agreement, gone after the iris to lure me away, and were trying to kill me."

Hellebore couldn't believe what she was hearing. This couldn't be possible. He was lying. He had to be. This was some elaborate scheme to cover up his treatment of her and his story didn't even make sense.

She turned on her heel, coming to a stop, and he stumbled back to avoid crashing into her as she jabbed a finger at his chest, staring up at him. She said, "If I knew you were my supposed betrothed and the king of the Sun Elves, would I really try to kill you and send us to war?"

"Yes." He crossed his arms. He wasn't that tall for an elf, and thankfully she was on the taller side for a woman, but he managed to make every inch he had on her count as he glared at her. "First off, you're human. Second, you're an alchemist. Third, you're a princess of Chymes. I absolutely believe you would try to kill me."

"First off, if I *was* trying to kill you, why would I have

sacrificed my escape to save you?" Her hand slapped her thigh as it dropped. "I gave you a sedative. Your reaction wasn't supposed to be that bad."

"Maybe you're not as great an alchemist as your reputation states, then."

Hellebore couldn't stop her lips from parting in a sharp gasp as he cut her to the core. She took a step back, tilting her head to keep her eyes locked on his. Immediately, his eyes widened and he took another step toward her, shaking his head, hands out. "Princess, look, this was all a misunderstanding. Clearly, a letter was lost or—or—something. Something went wrong somewhere, and we both made assumptions, and there's nothing to be done about it now. I can tell you what happened and what was supposed to happen. I asked your father for your hand in marriage. He agreed and led me to believe you had or would. I went to the academy to collect you and bring you here for our wedding where you would have been treated as my betrothed who was coming willingly, not a captive."

Hellebore grabbed the back of the sofa, taking a few shaky steps until she could drop onto it, her silk skirts tangling in her legs as she clutched the arm.

Her father had promised her hand to the Sun Elf king without a word to her and expected her to go along with it.

Of course he hadn't told her. She would have been out the window the second such a letter arrived with Palladia's blessing and promise to protect her location. But that didn't account for—

"Callahan—" She hated the way her brother's name cracked in her throat and came out as a breathy rasp. She hated the way King Taiyo stepped closer, eyes softening at the weakness. So she cleared her throat and hardened her voice. "My brother, Prince Callahan, he was present for this... agreement?"

King Taiyo came to a stop beside the chair closest to her. His voice was softer as he said, "He was. He was present for it all. He accepted my terms, including our marriage."

This wasn't supposed to happen. She wasn't supposed to be some pawn to be married off to secure alliances. She was the second born. She was meant to be Callahan's right hand. The King's Alchemist.

Her father had cared little for the tradition and more for politics, always wishing he'd had more daughters with hands he could trade away. She'd known that, but Callahan—

If he had agreed... it meant he didn't want her to be his alchemist. He didn't believe she was worthy of the title.

Could everyone else see through her supposed greatness but her and her aunt? Did everyone know Hellebore was an average alchemist at best?

How long had her brother been lying to her face and hiding the fact that he was looking for the first opportunity to have someone take her off his hands?

"I see." Hellebore took a deep breath. "And... the King's Alchemist, I know she wasn't there, but was she consulted?"

King Taiyo immediately scowled at the mention of Palladia, but his tone was restrained as he said, "I can't say with any certainty, given your father lied to my face about having spoken to you on the matter, but my terms included the King's Alchemist having no part of our discussion. Your father at least appeared eager to leave her out. When I arrived at the academy for you, I didn't stick around long enough to have any discourse with her, not that I would have even if you hadn't run off."

The elf didn't come any closer, but even if he did, Hellebore wasn't sure she would notice. Her voice came out of her mouth, but she had no awareness of speaking. It was like she was watching from the ramparts, a stranger in her own body, with no control over what happened next.

"Who... uh..." Her tongue was heavy and everything numb. "Was there a nobleman, an alchemist by the name of Emerson, my brother's friend—did he have any part in any of this?"

King Taiyo shook his head. "He might have been in the room, I don't recall. The only time his name was mentioned was by Prince Callahan saying Emerson would make an excellent King's Alchemist." He paused, shifting his weight as a strain entered his tone. "Did you... expect him to protest?"

Did she?

"No... No, I was... just curious who they wanted to succeed the King's Alchemist if... if not me," Hellebore said, gaze dropping to her hands. She'd been right. Things between her and Emerson hadn't been serious.

When she said nothing more, King Taiyo moved to sit in the chair, pulling it up to butt against the table and putting himself directly in front of her. When she looked up, she saw that he was pulling out a jar of salve and a roll of bandages from his pocket. He gestured to her wrists and said, "May I?"

Now he wanted to ask for permission? If she'd been in control of herself, she would have refused, but whatever strange, docile spirit that was possessing her would not let her go.

She held them out. He took the first one and she hissed as he applied the salve to her wrists. "My apologies, Princess, for your treatment. My guards' treatment of you only contributed to the situation, making you think we were enemies."

Hellebore didn't have the energy to expend to figure out

if he meant it or if he was just trying to placate her. Did it matter?

"I hit you with a trowel and accidentally poisoned you. How about we just call it even?" Hellebore said, lips twitching up in a smile so she didn't cry. There would be nothing worse than crying in front of an elf. No, actually, there would be nothing worse than crying in front of the elf who was insisting he was to be her husband after he'd dragged her to his castle kicking and screaming.

Taiyo looked up from her wrist and at her shoulder where a bruise peeked out past her collar. She wasn't expecting his hand to leave her wrist and gently pull at the fabric to expose the bruise to his eyes. Her breath caught in her throat as his warm, soft fingers traced the skin around the bruise, a darkness entering his eyes as he looked at the mark.

His voice was low, lips barely parting as he said, "They should not have treated their king's betrothed and their future queen as such. I commanded them to do you no harm even when you resisted."

Right. He may have thought initially that she was willing, but then he'd thought she'd run away and pursued her anyway. He thought she was willing to kill him to escape marrying him, and yet his plans had not changed a stitch. He didn't care if she agreed or not. He just wanted her to for his conscience. This marriage was happening regardless.

Her breath stuttered and she pressed herself back into the sofa as far as she could. His hand hovered in the air, and his lidded eyes lifted from the bruise, focusing in on her face.

Whatever he saw in her expression had him pulling his hand back, brow furrowing and scowling as he returned to her wrists.

Hellebore's heart was pounding in her chest and her

stomach was turning. She was just as much a captive against her will now as she had believed she'd been since she arrived. She had no say in this. This elf would do whatever he wanted with her. Her cooperation was a preference, not a requirement.

But she still let King Taiyo bandage her wrists.

As he finished her first wrist, he whispered, "Princess, this is not what either of us want—"

"Stop it. You don't have to put on an act." She narrowed her eyes as they met his, steeling her voice. If she was furious, she couldn't also be afraid. "Nothing has truly changed."

He frowned, eyes darting between her face and his hands as he began bandaging her other wrist. "I—I can move the ceremony back—not much, but enough time for you to send a letter. Hopefully long enough for you to come to terms with this—"

She ripped her second wrist out of his hands and moved to secure the bandage herself as she glared at him. "But letting me go isn't an option. It doesn't matter if it's tomorrow or two weeks or two months, the outcome is the same. My answer is a formality *you* can do without. You will force me to marry you."

His hands curled into fists as his brown eyes burned as bright as the fiery orange ends of his hair spilling off his shoulders. There. Apparently, what it took to crack his façade was the truth. He had no patience for his own foul deeds. He spat, "Do you think I want to marry a creature such as yourself?"

"With that tone, obviously not!" Hellebore dug her nails into the sofa, hoping it hid the way they were shaking. "Clearly, you have some other motivation here. Something obviously powerful enough to overcome your revulsion to humans and your hatred of alchemists. How could I ever hope to be able to dissuade you if those two things alone couldn't?"

"Will it help?" Taiyo's voice was frigid, sucking all the warmth out of the room.

Hellebore focused on each beat of her heart, echoing in her ears, the organ doubling as a metronome for her to cling to as her throat tightened. "What?"

"Everything my people think yours are, you believe about us in return, don't you?" Taiyo's lip curled into a sneer. "You think we're the monsters. You have to in order to be able to kidnap us to drain us of our blood just so you can find a new way to light a room because you aren't born with any real ability, just the power to manipulate ours."

"Neither of us were alive in those days. I went after a flower, not a person." Hellebore took a deep breath. "Now, do you *really* want to talk to me about kidnapping?"

Taiyo's jaw clenched as he leaned in. Every instinct in her screamed at her to move, but she stayed in her seat.

"Will it help if I act the part of the monster for you? Is that what you're looking for? Do you want to be a martyr in your mind?" His breath brushed her cheek as his hand braced against the back of the sofa, trapping her between him and the arm she was clutching. "If you make me be the villain, I will be."

Taiyo's eyes dropped to her lips, skimming over her dress before coming back to her eyes. "But I'd rather not be. It's up to you. Either way, I *will* be your husband."

"That is..." Hellebore's voice came out far breathier than she wanted it to, but she couldn't seem to make it any stronger with him so close. "That is precisely my point. Whether it is a few weeks or tomorrow, this ends the same way. So it doesn't matter if I try to refuse; it means nothing to you. So, to save us the trouble of delaying so you can pretend like you care about changing my mind, let's instead pretend as though I have any choice in the matter and we'll say I accept."

Taiyo pulled back, his hand dropping as he took her in. She hoped she wasn't shaking. That was second only to crying.

Once he'd studied her enough for his liking, he rose from his seat, brushing off his clothes. "I'm sorry it's come to this."

She shook her head and laughed. "No, you're not."

He took a deep breath, and the sparks from before almost rekindled, but they were gone as he exhaled. "I would not do this unless it was necessary. I know you may not believe me, but you and I are in the same position. Neither of us have a choice in this marriage."

Then he headed for the door.

She just stared at her bandaged wrists.

He was right; she didn't believe him.

When the door creaked open, she looked up. He paused in the doorway and looked back over his shoulder. He whispered, "Please, don't make this more difficult than it needs to be."

He should have thought about that before deciding to marry an alchemist.

But she was tired and her shoulders still hurt, and she desperately wanted to run to her aunt and ask her how this could have possibly happened. She wanted to grab Callahan and scream at him for betraying her like this. While she was many things, she was not going to start a war because she wasn't as good an alchemist as she'd believed herself to be.

It was a miracle she hadn't started one accidentally, and she would certainly not start one on purpose.

"I'll see you at the wedding, Your Majesty."

Then he was gone, and Hellebore pressed her fist to her mouth as the tears welled up, refusing to let them fall. She would not cry.

If this was her fate, she would bear it well.

But even that, she failed to achieve.

CHAPTER 6

ellebore was dozing on the sofa, sleeve stained with tears, evidence of her weakness and unsuitability to be the next King's Alchemist, when a knock sounded on the door.

She scrubbed her cheeks and called out, "Yes?"

The door creaked open and it was the two servant girls from before, one carrying the potted Sunrise Iris and the other a dinner tray.

"From His Majesty, Your Highness," the first one said, holding out the pot with a note attached to a ribbon tied around the pot.

Hellebore rose from her seat as the second girl set the tray on the table. It seemed as though these two maids were going to be permanently assigned to her. They were both pretty, as almost all elves were. The taller one was of a fairer skin tone, more closely matching Hellebore's than Taiyo's, and she had blonde hair that faded into a soft pink. The other one had a warm, light brown skin tone and a wide smile, her hair brown mixed with shimmering gold. If they were going to be sticking around, Hellebore supposed she'd better get used to it and use them.

Hellebore took the plant and asked, "Just so I know, how old are the two of you?"

"I'm Phoebe, Your Highness. I just turned forty." The taller of the two gestured to herself with a smile before pointing to the other. Although both were taller than Hellebore. "Elaine is thirty-five."

Hellebore did not return the smile. Her voice was still clipped and cold. "Which would make you how old if you were human?"

Phoebe and Elaine exchanged a look, seeming to speak to each other in the silence before Phoebe said, "I'd say we're roughly around your age."

Hellebore picked at the ribbon tied around the pot. "And King Taiyo?"

"Oh, he's only fifty-six," Elaine said. "Which I believe if you were counting in human years, that makes him around twenty-eight?"

Phoebe laughed. "That sounds so young to our ears."

She supposed that made sense. Her father had been thirty-two when he married her mother, who'd been a few years older than Hellebore was now. Besides, Taiyo was an elf and this was clearly a political match, so it wasn't ideal, but it wasn't repulsive to her. Rather, it wasn't his age that was repulsive to her. It did at least put things into perspective.

She was a temporary thing to him. He'd live at least another century and a half after her death.

To him, she was a brief indignity to suffer through and once she was gone, he could marry an elf and have his heirs and spare his country from war without having to subject his people to half-human heirs—or worse, an alchemist.

"Of course, thank you," Hellebore murmured as she set

the plant down and allowed the maids to help her out of the dress and into a nightgown.

As they went to leave, she caught Phoebe and said, "Bring me any books you have in the library on Iubian Elvish and Chymesian."

Phoebe startled, eyes widening. "But Your Highness, your wedding is tomorrow. You need to sleep."

"I just want to make sure I get through that first. My Iubian..." Hellebore gestured in the air, indicating her accent.

The two maids exchanged another look, this one indecipherable to Hellebore. But then they turned back to her and nodded in perfect unison before scurrying off to meet her request. She wandered back to the table to eat, digging in while she opened the note attached to the Sunrise Iris.

In an elegant script was:

Hellebore,

I see now that you did not have any idea of the significance of uprooting and taking a Sunrise Iris. These plants are quite sacred to my people. We never take them from the ground, but for one occasion. The day before his wedding, a groom goes on a quest to find one, and if he is successful, he gifts it to his bride on their wedding night. It is a sign of fortune over their union, and of the utmost importance to care for it the way they are called to care for their spouse and their marriage. Finding them has become few and far between for many elves as of late. Despite the fact that you are the one who found it, and I'm gifting it to you now, I hope that it might still be a sign of good fortune for our union.

Into your care I trust this iris.

Yours,

Taiyo

Hellebore glared at the glowing flower. But she still found a spot in the sunlight for it.

Her husband-to-be had no idea what she was. She wasn't a botanist. She didn't have a green thumb.

Her only interest in the iris had been how quickly she could rot it from the inside out.

* * *

Phoebe and Elaine returned with the requested books and to take away the dinner tray once Hellebore was done with it. Hellebore snatched the books from the maids and started to head for the bed to dive in when Elaine cleared her throat.

"Your Highness, do you want these letters?"

Hellebore looked over her shoulder to see the girl wasn't holding up Taiyo's note to her, but a different sized envelope entirely. She must have missed it before. She reached out and took it wordlessly as the maids bid her a good night.

She bit her tongue. What was so good about it being the last night before her fate was truly sealed?

Instead, she set aside the books and turned over the envelope, heart stopping at the seal.

The Chymesian royal seal.

There were only two options. Her father or Callahan.

Hellebore broke it as she clambered onto the bed, leaning close to the candlelight to read by.

One glance at the handwriting smashed her hopes. It was her father's handwriting.

Hellebore,

You understand by now what it is that's expected of you. However, in case it wasn't clear, or you have doubts whether you can trust King Taiyo's word, I will make it plain again. He will be your husband. You will go with him to Auror where you will be married.

Hellebore snorted. If only her father had had the foresight that she wouldn't get the chance to read this until she'd already been forcibly carried off to Auror.

There will be no arguing. I will be hearing no protests, not from you or my sister. The decision has been made, and King Taiyo will be leaving with you before the end of the day. He has my permission to use whatever means necessary should you fail to see reason and cooperate.

While that alone should be sufficient, I will continue as necessary to cover all objections.

I am aware of the rumors of a flirtation you were having with Callahan's friend, Emerson. Don't think I didn't know the second it started. The only reason it happened was because I allowed it to happen. While I could tell it was simply the foolish passion of youth on his end, I permitted it because of his good breeding, skill in alchemy, and loyalty to Callahan. I could have forced the match at any point should no better options have come along.

When one did, I had no qualms about accepting it. I watched him closely as he and Callahan attended the meetings, and he did not speak out once. He did not so much as break a sweat. There was no fear or concern in his expression. And if that wasn't enough, I had Callahan confirm it with him— Emerson saw you as a pretty way to pass the time at the academy when his studies weren't challenging enough to keep his attention. He never entertained any serious affection for you.

He will make an excellent King's Alchemist for Callahan; of that, there is no doubt. It is a great reassurance to me to have him secured for the position. Had this opportunity not arisen...

Hellebore had suspected as much, but reading it still sent a sharp rolling wave through her stomach. She wasn't foolish enough to believe Emerson had loved her, but he hadn't even cared enough about her to at least pretend they had a secret engagement to try to stop this? She'd thought if nothing else, they were friends enough for him to at least say something on her behalf.

Maybe they had been, but maybe he saw the opportunity to take the most coveted position in all the kingdom and he wanted that more. Why be the husband of the King's Alchemist when now he could *be* the King's Alchemist?

There's really no delicate way to put it. You're more useful to Chymes as a bride than an alchemist. My sister's fondness of you blinds her, but I am not so fooled. I have kept track of your studies and while your teachers have taken pity on you or feared Palladia, it's clear your work was only passable at best.

While your status as a princess only puffed up your ego and hindered any progress you might have made as an alchemist, at least you have other uses. A pretty enough face that hopefully your husband finds more exotic than repulsive. A dowry large enough to make up for the case of the latter.

The ability to do as you're told.

Should you think you don't possess that quality, you'd better acquire it with haste.

There is no other option. You will marry King Taiyo. You have no choice.

Should you be mistaken and believe you do and try to refuse, you will discover the consequences. If you attempt to remain in Chymes or try to return to Chymes without marrying the king, you will be treated like the traitor those actions would make you. Chymes' treaty and future with Iubar is sealed by your marriage. To defy that is an act of treason, and I will not let such actions go unpunished.

There is nothing for you in Chymes but a noose.

I take no pleasure in such pronouncements, but I will not repeat mistakes. I tell you this only so you understand the gravity of this matter. I hope my sister has not made you so entirely into her image that you would be unable to grasp that.

You will not write to anyone in Chymes of your own accord. Do not think you are cleverer than you are. You will not be arranging an escape that way. All mail travelling from Iubar and into Chymes will be checked and should anything have your name alone, it will be destroyed. However, should you have anything of actual importance to write about, you may send it through your new husband. His approval will ensure your letters are not destroyed and there is nothing in them you would not want him to see.

Don't be foolish. Don't embarrass Chymes. Be grateful for the opportunity to be useful to your country. Forget about alchemy. Be a good wife.

King Silas

Hellebore was tempted to stick the edges of the pages into the candle's flame and let it all go up. It would likely catch the whole room on fire if she did and put an end to the whole affair before it began.

She didn't.

What would be the use?

Instead, she folded the pages back up and set them on the nightstand before blowing out the candle beside her. Once the flame was out, her books on Iubian Elvish forgotten on the table, she sank into the blankets again. The only light was the slight glow of the Sunrise Iris' bloom.

Hellebore covered her mouth with her hand, but it didn't make a difference.

The tears came anyway. No matter how hard she tried not to feel, her father's words circled in on her, only they were in Callahan's voice.

If Callahan hadn't fought for her to remain in Chymes, then it meant he believed all of it too.

Hellebore turned on her side, burying her head into the pillow, using it to muffle her sob. She gave in. She'd let it all out.

Once she was done crying, she would be done mourning. She would be done feeling.

When the sun rose, she would remain numb. She would be perfectly cold. Eternally calculating. It was the only way she was going to survive her so-called marriage.

CHAPTER 7

Hellebore was surrounded by a fleet of serving girls and seamstresses—headed up by Phoebe and Elaine—after being woken up at the crack of dawn on her wedding day to begin preparations. This time, however, she was content to let them do whatever they wished so long as they did not disturb the Chymesian to Iubian dictionary in her hand. Since being woken up, she'd been refreshing herself to hopefully make conversations smoother, but she still had a while to go before she could be considered fluent.

Hellebore felt nothing but the smooth pages beneath her fingertips. There was nothing but calm acceptance. She was many things, but she was not going to rage or mourn in futility. Her fate was sealed. Better to get on with it.

Hellebore flipped a page, causing the seamstress on her right to prick her and chide her right as the door opened and all the girlish chatter ceased. Hellebore lifted her eyes from her page to see the female elf from before, the one wearing the royal pattern, King Taiyo's sister, Hellebore presumed. They looked alike, both having that warm, amber-toned skin, brown eyes, and black hair that faded into orange. She had an elfling on her hip as she stood in the doorframe, a stern, commanding presence despite the baby trying to take her necklace and stick the rubies in his mouth to drool on.

Hellebore had not spent much time with babies in Chymes, but it was nice to see that there were at least some similarities in the way babies conducted themselves across species.

"Your Highness," the servants and seamstresses murmured as she strode into the room.

Hellebore kept her arm holding her book aloft, given the number of pins in the sleeve that was currently being sewn together while on her.

Like politics, decorum had never been Hellebore's area either, so since she hadn't been given a formal introduction to Taiyo's sister, she was unsure what the expectation was.

"Alchemist, my brother has been unexpectedly occupied this morning, so I took it upon myself to facilitate our introduction."

Hellebore was lucky the translation for "facilitate" was on the page she had open.

"I am Princess Haruko, His Majesty's older sister, your soon-to-be sister-in-law." The way Haruko said it made it clear she did not find that to be a cause for celebration.

Was there anybody in Iubar who was excited about the union? Why had King Taiyo wanted her hand in the first place?

"Lovely to make your acquaintance. You already know who I am, so now we are on equal ground."

Princess Haruko stepped farther into the room, the maids scattering to get out of her way. She looked at the seamstresses and said, "Continue on, we cannot delay."

The seamstresses obeyed and continued sewing Hellebore into the dress.

Haruko came to a stop in front of Hellebore, just behind the seamstresses, and took her in. Haruko and Taiyo both weren't as tall as some of the other elves, but both were taller than Hellebore and the average human.

Her eyes landed on the book in Hellebore's hand and she raised an eyebrow. "My brother said your Iubian was subpar."

Hellebore's fingers curled in tighter on the dictionary. Oh, had he?

"His Chymesian has room for improvement. Actually, his communication in either language leaves a lot to be desired."

There were a few stifled gasps from the serving girls who had been trying very hard to make it seem like their pointed ears couldn't hear anything more than an inch away from them.

"Still, it is a pleasant surprise to see you deigning to improve your skills in our tongue. Not what I expected from someone like you."

"Right. Because a human alchemist would have no interest in learning anything," Hellebore sneered.

"I meant a relation of Palladia."

Hellebore knew her aunt had met King Taiyo twenty-five years ago, and knowing now his age and the corresponding development of elves, Taiyo had been incredibly young for a king. Clearly her aunt had not left a favorable impression on Taiyo's sister either. But what could her aunt have done to give such a specific impression? She was an alchemist; the pursuit of knowledge was in their blood.

"Is there anything I can help you with, Princess? I'm a little busy today," Hellebore said, pointedly looking at the seamstresses around her and lowering her voice. "Who knew marrying a king would be *such* an ordeal?"

The elfling on Haruko's hip successfully got the chain of the necklace into his gummy, toothless mouth, and Hellebore hoped she hadn't been planning on wearing it for the ceremony.

"I am here to make things crystal clear to you since my brother is far kinder than I am."

Taiyo was supposed to be the kind one?

Hellebore couldn't help her snort, but Haruko ignored her and pressed on. "You are a necessary evil. You are—"

"A human. Worse, an alchemist. Thank you so much for reminding me." Hellebore's lips twitched into a sardonic grin, but she was completely empty on the inside. "Spending the night here and wearing your people's clothes made me almost forget I'm not an elf."

Strangely enough, Haruko wasn't charmed. She adjusted her grip on her baby and stepped closer. "Don't get smart with me."

"If my aunt and my reputation precede me, then you know I can't be anything less. I'm a most accomplished alchemist." At least, Hellebore would maintain she was publicly even if no one else agreed.

"You are here to serve a purpose. You might wear the title of queen for a brief, fleeting moment, but you will not last. You will be a footnote, not a legacy."

Hellebore glanced at the elfling and nodded. "And I take it I am looking at the one who will be carrying on the royal line if you have your way? He is a full-blooded elf, right?"

"Your pride over your own ignorance is a particularly appalling trait, but I should have expected as much from one of your kind. You do know Queen Idonea of the Star Elves will be in attendance today?"

Hellebore had heard the news of the Star Elf king

getting married recently, but what it had to do with her marriage, she didn't know. It did grate against her skin though that apparently it was something she was supposed to know and that it was relevant to Haruko but she had no idea how.

"Queen Idonea is only half-elf." Haruko hefted her son up higher on her hip. "You don't know anything about me, my opinions, or what way I would have if I could. Your marriage to my brother will not last long."

Even if Hellebore maintained perfect health, their marriage would only last about sixty years, giving Taiyo a little more than half of his remaining lifetime to be free from her.

"Look, Princess, stop stating obvious facts." Hellebore turned slightly, facing Haruko fully as best she could without earning the seamstresses' ire. "Sarcasm aside, we have a very important wedding happening in a few hours despite how much we both wish otherwise."

Haruko's voice was as stiff and cold as steel. "You almost killed my brother once already."

Were they ever going to let that go?

"It was an *accident*. I was sedating him." Hellebore huffed, rolling her eyes and getting stabbed in the shoulder when she moved, tilting her head and adding, "And I saved him, by the way, too, but that doesn't fit in your neat little narrative about evil alchemists."

"Don't hurt him again."

Then Princess Haruko tugged the chain of her necklace out of her baby's mouth and swept away toward the door. She paused by the nightstand where Hellebore had placed the iris so it sat in the sunlight.

However, she said nothing in acknowledgment and just walked out of the room.

Hellebore lifted her chin and let the seamstresses finish sewing her into her wedding dress.

Good. The shallow fits and spurts of frustration hadn't overtaken her. Not even her combative future sister-in-law had broken the pervasive numbness she'd shrouded herself in.

CHAPTER 8

The wedding was scheduled to start at high noon when the Sun Elves' strength and energy were at their peak.

Hellebore had her skirts gathered up in her arms as she rushed down the halls, following Phoebe and Elaine the second her hair had been finished. She was pretty sure there were still a few pins holding the elaborate dress together that were absolutely going to scratch her, but they were already about to be late.

She huffed for breath as they raced down the last staircase, and her skirts slipped out of her grip, tangling her legs. She pitched forward, scrambling to grab the railing. A pair of hands wrapped around her back and she was steadied against something solid but far too warm to be a wall.

She looked up to see King Taiyo on the last step, having rushed to catch her.

"Your Majesty—" Phoebe started.

He was staring down at Hellebore and didn't break her gaze as he said, "Thank you, Phoebe, for delivering her to

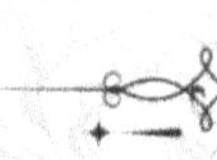

me. That will be all for now."

Hellebore's hands were on his shoulders, gripping his shirt. It was a smooth, fine silk, the color and pattern matching her bodice.

She didn't like the way he was still looking at her, holding her against himself, so she said, "Don't blame me for being late. Your sister interrupted."

His hands shifted across her back, letting her straighten up and get her balance again but not pulling away fully. "You're not too late. Not yet. There's still time."

She also didn't like the weight to his words. She pulled her hands back and grabbed the railing as he stepped backward to the flat floor, eyes still not leaving her face.

"Then I suppose we'd better get on with it while there is still time."

"Hellebore..." His voice lowered. "Are you certain?"

It took all of her self-control not to find one of the little sharp pins digging into her side and stab him with it. How dare he act like he was giving her some kind of say in the matter when he had no intention of ever letting her go?

She glared at him. "You are. Isn't that all that matters?"

"I'm not doing this to make you miserable."

"I know. You're doing this because there's no other choice and you're a king and I'm a princess before I'm an alchemist and these are the things we do to serve our people." She still didn't know what he'd originally meant when he'd claimed he had no choice either, but she supposed seconds before the ceremony wasn't the time to get into all of that. "You, however, are going to blink and I'll be dead, so it's not that much of a hardship, is it?"

Taiyo snorted, lips twisting in a pained, sardonic smile. "I doubt that."

Then he took another step back, letting her come down the last step. He looked at her fully, taking her in in her wedding dress, eyes softening. The silks and style were completely foreign to her, enveloping her in soft dusky pinks and oranges, embroidered with gold. All of it matched his outfit. He wasn't outright recoiling at the sight; her maids and seamstresses had at least made her into the image of something acceptable to him.

He took a deep breath and looped his arm through hers and nodded at the footmen waiting at the doors. Apparently, it was Sun Elf custom for the bride and groom to walk to the altar together.

She lifted her chin and straightened her shoulders as Taiyo took a deep breath while the doors opened and they faced their fate.

It was hard to put on a smile and pretend he was walking with her when the truth was he was dragging her.

* * *

Hellebore had only seen a couple of Chymesian weddings in her lifetime and never a Sun Elf one before.

But Phoebe and Elaine had given her a quick briefing on what to expect and what was expected of her, so she was adequately prepared.

There was quite a crowd assembled, the majority Sun Elves—nobles, she presumed. But there were a few that were quite clearly not Sun Elves, given their differences in appearance and in their favored colors. Given the rising tension between the Sun Elves and the Moon Elves, she ruled them out quickly, leaving the only other option as the Star Elves. A few of them were in the crowd, marked by the hues of purple and blue in their hair and their clothes that were adorned with silver, shining patterns of stars.

Hellebore pulled her gaze away. She needed to focus on making sure she didn't make a fool of herself.

They reached the officiant and stepped inside the circle of orange, gold, and pink petals scattered across the courtyard and beneath an arch of matching flowers. Taiyo held her arm and helped her kneel without falling over before he took his spot, kneeling across from her.

Something was... off. There was a tension in the air. All because the king was marrying a human? It wasn't that wildly far from imagination since there was a half-elf queen in the courtyard among the Star Elves.

Could it be just because she was an alchemist? Possibly.

Still, even for a monarch's wedding, there were a lot more guards than expected. Maybe she should be flattered they thought she was enough of a threat to warrant such measures. Although, she was probably sharing that honor with the Moon Elves.

But even that didn't quite fully account for the sense of unease she had as the officiant launched into his speech. Before she could figure it out, she had to drop it and focus on translating so she didn't get lost.

She kept her palms flat on her knees, ignoring the glare Princess Haruko gave her from the front row, sitting beside her husband, her son dozing on her lap.

There was much Hellebore needed to get to the bottom of if this was to be her fate.

After the wedding.

There were several strange things that were part of the ceremony that were not part of Chymesian weddings. The officiant sprinkling petals over their heads was one. The use of magic was another.

Right before their vows, the two Sun Elves typically both used their sun magic to create a halo matching the circle on the ground, weaving sunlight between the two of them as they rose to take each other's hands.

It would be Taiyo's sole responsibility, unless of course, they wanted to offer her up some Sun Elf blood so she could access the magic in it. That was so far off the table, Hellebore hadn't even brought it up as a joke. She didn't want to ruin what little good standing she had with her maids.

The time for the vows came, and Taiyo began using his magic, sunlight obeying his command.

She was riveted by it. He'd had a point. As an alchemist, all she could do was manipulate. She couldn't create.

"In the light of the sun and before the eyes of my people as my witness, I take Princess Hellebore of Chymes to be my wife, to love, honor, and protect, for as long as we both..." Taiyo paused and the sunlight stuttered.

Hellebore's eyes widened. Was he having second thoughts?

He took another breath and the sunlight weaving through the air brightened. "For as long as we both shall live."

Once the strands of sunlight hung in the air, wrapping around them, not quite blinding but almost, the novelty wore off as the heat began to get under her skin and aggravate her along with the pins she was certain were starting to leave pinpricks of blood on her shift beneath the dress. Taiyo held his hands out to her. She took them and let him help her to her feet.

"Princess Hellebore," the officiant said.

"In the light of the sun and before the eyes of these people—" She ignored the sharpening of Haruko's glare, but Hellebore would not lie. None of her people were present as witnesses. "—as my witness, I take King Taiyo to be my husband to love, honor, and protect for as long as we both shall live."

Taiyo's hands holding hers shifted, not letting go but moving his fingers enough for the sunlight to dance, reaching blinding brightness as the officiant said, "I pronounce you husband and wife. You may kiss the bride."

Thankfully no one would be able to see when Taiyo didn't—

But then his hands tugged hers closer and he leaned down. She was blinded by the light, but his lips brushed her cheek before he let it dim.

She shifted back, blinking furiously to clear her vision so she could glare at him. What had that been for?

He gave her a small smile and squeezed her hands as the crowd politely applauded before he started to lead her back down the aisle.

Hellebore looked back over her shoulder.

That was when it hit her.

Everything looked beautiful and full of life, but there was something in the air. She took a deep breath, finding the faintest foul hint, nearly buried beneath the overwhelming floral scents flooding the air. She knew it well enough from behind a mask that she would be able to recognize it anywhere.

Something was rotting.

CHAPTER 9

Hellebore sat beside her new husband in the middle of a long table, facing the rest of the ball-room where the guests sat eating.

There were quite a few exotic foods on her plate that would normally interest her simply for the fact that of discovering if there could be an alchemic use for them, but she was preoccupied.

Taiyo was silent, eating quietly while his sister sat on his other side. Haruko was thankfully too busy helping her husband entertain the nobles and keeping their son from growing fussy to keep up her glare at Hellebore.

There wasn't much opportunity for Hellebore to speak to Taiyo anyway as every few minutes another noble was let through to pay their respects to their king and his new queen consort.

Hellebore didn't miss the strain in their smiles or slight pauses before addressing her or acknowledging her.

Queen Hellebore.

Ugh. She hated the sound of it.

"King Nyrunn and Queen Idonea of the Star Elves," the

herald announced, and this was one visit Hellebore did want to pay attention to.

King Nyrunn and Queen Idonea approached and Hellebore set down her glass of wine, sitting up a little straighter at their approach. King Nyrunn inclined his head respectfully. "Congratulations, Your Majesty, on your wedding, and I hope your new alliance with Chymes is prosperous."

Taiyo nodded his acceptance and started talking, but Hellebore was focused on the only creature somewhat close to her kind.

"Queen Idonea, it is an honor to have you at my wedding," Hellebore said, catching the half-elf slightly off guard. She wasn't nearly as good at masking her emotions as her husband beside her.

Idonea gave her a soft smile, but her eyes were somehow both curious and old. "This is a historic occasion. Despite the short notice, my husband and I had to come witness it. I have somewhat of an interest in history, and for a formal marriage alliance between the Sun Elves and the alchemists? I know of little else that matches that."

"Ah, so you came to make sure the big bad alchemist princess didn't steal his blood and magic during the ceremony?" Hellebore gave a light laugh.

Next to her, Taiyo stuttered over his words, but otherwise was immersed in his conversation with King Nyrunn.

Idonea didn't seem to find the joke as amusing, as she eyed the knife on Hellebore's plate and said, "Something like that."

Not even the half-human was sympathetic.

Then again, historically the Star Elves had always aligned with the witches against the alchemists, so they weren't her allies either.

No one was.

"I'm honored everyone thinks so highly of my intelligence and skill in alchemy that I could be capable of such a feat as killing my husband at the altar." Hellebore laughed, clinging to the cold numbness. At least the elves thought she was skilled enough to be feared. "Really, I don't know what I've done to earn such respect."

A hand landed on her knee, squeezing it even as the owner was still intently listening to King Nyrunn.

A warning.

Her heel slamming into his ankle caused him to startle and wince, drawing Idonea's attention and cutting Nyrunn off mid-sentence. Hellebore smirked as she lifted her glass to her lips while Taiyo made an excuse about banging his knee into the leg of the table.

When the other monarchs left, he fixed his gaze on her and lowered his voice. "Was that necessary?"

Through her wide, fake smile, she replied in Iubian, "Since no one ever taught you to keep your hands to yourself, yes."

Taiyo raised an eyebrow. "And you were taught that such macabre, treasonous jokes were appropriate?"

"You know..." Hellebore leaned in closer, voice soft but sharp as she gave him a cold grin. "I think that was the lesson right behind the one about kings who kidnap their brides and treat them like prisoners."

Taiyo scoffed, sitting back in his seat. "And here I thought you might want to enter our marriage with a fresh start, given your hands aren't clean either."

"Don't mistake my acquiescence for agreeableness. Maybe I'll get over it when you get over the sedative and thank me for saving your life."

"Spent the morning brushing up on your vocabulary? Soon you'll be fluent. That seems agreeable to me. But no, I don't see myself thanking you for botching your escape and nearly killing me in the process anytime soon."

"Then maybe I should have left you there. The great Sun Elf king killed by a little princess playing alchemist. It'd be the start to a bloodier war than any in history, but if you're the Sun Elves' leader and representative of Iubar's strength, then I like my chances."

Taiyo shook his head and looked back out at the crowd, that pained smile from before returning, but there was no light in his eyes. She heard him mutter, "This was a mistake."

Oh, now he was regretting it?

He couldn't have thought that last night?

It was then that music started up, and she did her best to restrain a sigh while Taiyo's brow pinched. Haruko gave them a pointed look, and Taiyo rose from his seat, holding his hand out to Hellebore, and said, "Our dance?"

She ignored it and pushed herself out of her seat and said, "If we must."

Although, what she really needed were answers. Maybe it was time to get them.

Her skirts billowed around her as she followed Taiyo to the dance floor where he gave her a stern look and she let him take her hand and set his in the proper position on her waist. He'd at least chosen a dance they had in Chymes that she knew.

Of course, because elves had magic, they had to show off with it as well. So that was why Taiyo's fingers on her waist kept shifting slightly to twirl the threads of sunlight he left in their wake as they began moving. Hellebore understood the necessity of the spectacle as part of the Sun Elves' traditions, but the feel of his fingers darting against her side was maddening in its distraction.

She wasn't an excellent dancer in the first place, so if she was going to live up to expectations and not embarrass herself as well as interrogate her husband, she needed to focus.

Her hand rested on his shoulder, and she spoke beneath the music, keeping her eyes on the crowd. "You may at any point, but preferably now, inform me why you're doing this. I still don't understand why having me would be in any way a victory for you."

"You make me sound like a monster."

"Pardon, I forgot. That's supposed to be me, isn't it?" Hellebore ducked under his arm as he spun her before pulling her back in. She looked up at him. "Which again simply proves my point, and yet all you do is avoid answering."

"You're the one who had no interest in any discussion and insisted upon moving forward in ignorance."

Hellebore let out a scoff as his sunlight kept weaving a path behind them. "Like you would have been honest with me when there was a chance I could find a way out. I saw through your façade and didn't waste our time. You were determined to marry me at any cost. You slung me over your shoulder and threw me in a carriage."

Taiyo's jaw clenched, but he said nothing.

"But now... You've got me. There will be no escaping on my end anymore. You win," Hellebore said right before he spun her out again and pulled her back in, this time her back to his front and his arms encircling her. She looked up at him from the corner of her eye and whispered, "But what exactly did you win? I'm not a fool. What did you do all of this for? You can't have lowered yourself and gone to all this effort just because you think the Moon Elves are a little antsy. What is this really about? Revenge? The desire to humiliate an alchemist? Something to do with whatever you're hiding on these grounds that is rotting to death?"

His eyes widened, and instead of finishing the move properly, he shoved her away from him.

It had been the last move of the dance anyway. She recovered easily enough and flashed a smile at a crowd that at best feared her and at worst wanted her to drop dead. Most wanted both.

Then a hand brushed the small of her back and she watched Taiyo recover, stepping up behind her and smiling at his people, who finally applauded for his sake. His breath brushed over her ear as his hand clenched into the fabric of her dress. "Believe me, I'm not trying to humiliate you. As much as revenge might be justified, I would rather have nothing to do with your kind ever again."

So it was the last.

Then his hand slipped into hers. The sun had just started to set.

"Come with me."

She let him take her hand if it would get her answers, and it was better than him hovering over her and causing her heart to race from hypervigilance.

* * *

Hellebore kept up with Taiyo as he led her out to the courtyard again. She took a deep breath and the faint scent of rot returned.

Everything was painted in a stunning, ethereal golden glow of the sunset, but her new husband did not seem to enjoy the view, especially since the setting sun ebbed his energy and strength.

But Hellebore's energy came rushing back all anew with the promise of answers and a dying specimen. If there was something dying, she wanted to have her hands on it. Alchemists always learned the most when they studied the dying.

It didn't matter what her father ordered in his letter.

She could no sooner forget about alchemy than she could forget about breathing.

Taiyo, however, didn't lead her into the courtyard but along the wall of the palace until they reached another small door, hidden in the shadow of a large shrub. Taiyo pulled out a key and unlocked it before reaching back and pulling her into the passage, swiftly shutting and locking it.

The only explanation he offered was, "I'm the only one with the key."

"I hope you mean to wherever this passageway leads, because otherwise, I'd hardly consider this something worthy of a king's attention."

Taiyo snorted as he held one hand out, creating tendrils of sunlight to illuminate the corridor before he took her hand in his other and pulled her along.

Shortly they stepped back outside again and into a courtyard, but this one was much smaller than the garden they'd been married in. She looked up to see it was expertly hidden, the terrain and the hedges all perfectly arranged so that none of the windows above could peer down into it. A private courtyard.

Hellebore could smell the rot before she saw the source. Taiyo sent his sunlight into the space as they stepped out into it.

It wasn't a garden. It was a graveyard.

All save for one sole surviving patch that was still clinging to life in the middle of the garden. Amidst the dead plants and decay was a patch of Sunrise Irises.

She took a few more steps, feeling the silent weight of Taiyo's gaze on her. She looked at them, analyzing, and even they weren't untouched by whatever disease had taken hold of the space. A few of their leaves were yellowing. She looked at all the death and decay coating the ground in brown and black. She gestured at the remains as she looked back at Taiyo. "Were these all Sunrise Irises?"

He nodded, jaw tightly clenched.

When he said nothing, she whispered, "What happened?"

He stared at her for a moment before slowly unclenching his jaw. He gestured to the side of the garden closest to the castle and farthest from the still living patch. "Some time ago, the irises started rotting here first, slowly. We've done everything we can to save this garden. When that failed, we tried to protect the irises it hadn't spread to. Six months ago, the last healthy patch there caught it. Years ago, one of our enemies introduced the disease and it's been slowly spreading throughout Iubar ever since."

"It's affecting your whole kingdom," Hellebore's voice softened. "When I crossed the border, I saw a few flowers that were sick and rotting before I found the iris."

He nodded.

"And this..." Hellebore gestured, feeling a little out of place amidst the decay in her vibrant wedding dress. "This is why you married me?"

"You were right. It wasn't just because of the Moon Elves starting to move aggressively. In ordinary circumstances, we would be equipped to handle them. These circumstances are far from it. Neither I nor the most skilled of my kingdom have been able to use any means magical or mundane to stop this rot. The eclipse is coming. The Star Elves successfully strengthened their magic with the passing of their comet last year, which only leaves us the weakest link."

"So while this whole marriage was your idea..." Hellebore took in a sharp breath. "This is what you meant by not having a choice?"

"This eclipse, we'll be weaker and more vulnerable than

we've ever been. In the past, we strengthened ourselves and survived eclipses by having the Sunrise Irises to bolster us. Without them, and a weak, poisoned land..." Taiyo's shoulders shifted back as he gestured at the mess. "You see the predicament."

Hellebore looked around once again. And then she laughed.

It overtook her whole body as she devolved into hysteria. This. This was what she'd been ripped from her home, from her future, from everything she'd worked so hard to achieve, for. This was why she'd been thrown over his shoulder and dragged kicking and screaming and why he would not have ever let her go.

She stumbled back and hands grabbed her, trying to keep her upright, but she brought them both to the ground, crushing her skirts and getting the dirt and decay all over the vivid orange and soft pinks as tears spilled out from her eyes as she kept laughing.

"Hellebore? Hellebore!"

Then she caught herself on Taiyo's shoulders as he knelt in front of her. She did her best to control her laughter, muffling it with her hand as she said, "You did all of this to me not because you needed a wife, but because you need an alchemist. You stole me, have secured my vow and have taken my hand and the rest of my life from me, because you, King Taiyo of the Sun Elves, need an *alchemist* to save you."

His hands tightened on her shoulders and he jostled her slightly, glaring at her. "Hellebore! If I had any other option left, I would have taken it."

She couldn't help her snort as she leaned forward and took his face in her hands, beaming at him as she said, "Oh, I *know*, and that's what makes this so wonderful. You came crawling to my kingdom, desperate, begging for the help of your greatest enemy. Only you were so prideful, you couldn't admit it and instead hid it behind the guise of a marriage alliance. You were willing to lower yourself to marrying a creature you despise just as much as you need. And you hate yourself for it."

He snapped, "And what about this is so joyful to you?"

"You might have trapped me and bound me to you for the rest of my life, but it's not going to be as a wife in anything but name. You need a King's Alchemist. I can be your alchemist, and I take great delight in how much you need my skills when you hate me for them."

Taiyo stared at her for a moment before reaching up and taking her wrists, still a little red, brushing his thumb softly over her pulse and whispering, "Please, Hellebore."

She took another look around then back at her husband. "Lucky for you, I do so love rotting things. And I'll need something to occupy my time. I'll do it."

And then to her surprise, he pulled her into his chest, crushing her to himself as if she'd taken a great weight off him.

This might not be the king she'd had in mind, but she'd been born to be a King's Alchemist. Much more than she'd been born to be a wife or a queen. Plus, it was so satisfying to have a Sun Elf begging for an alchemist's help.

CHAPTER 10

Hellebore's mind was already spinning with where she would start. The second Taiyo's grip on her slackened, she pulled away, ready to get started, but Taiyo did not relinquish her fully. He pulled her to her feet and forced her gaze to his.

"While I appreciate the enthusiasm, we've both had a rather exhausting time as of late, and we disappeared from our own reception. Not to mention the stench—" Taiyo coughed, shaking his head before he gently pulled her toward the exit. "You can start first thing in the morning."

Hellebore looked down at her dress, dirt and decay smeared on the skirts. "I'm not going back to that reception looking like this."

Taiyo's hand was on the small of her back as he ushered her into the passageway. "When did I say we were going back to the reception?"

Oh, perfect. Hellebore wanted out of the ridiculous dress anyway; it was a miracle she hadn't bled through it with all the pins stabbing her.

The castle was quiet, as most everyone was either in the

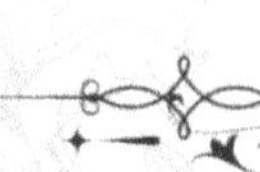

ballroom attending the reception or nearby serving the reception. They passed by a few guards and servants, but not many. Hellebore was more focused on locating the pin digging into her hip than them. Taiyo, however, stiffened every time they spotted an elf and his pace increased. Hellebore was left to lengthen her stride and pick up her pace so as not to be left behind. If she lost him, she'd have no idea how to find her room.

Finally, they made it to her hallway, and Hellebore had successfully removed three of the pins that had been driving her up the wall as Taiyo opened her door.

She looked up from the pin in her hand, mouth open to thank him for the escort, but he had already entered, still holding onto the door and waiting on her.

She curled her fingers over the pins and slowly entered her room. He must want to continue their discussion where it didn't reek of rot as much.

That better be all he was after.

Once she was back in her room, he shut the door behind her, and she turned on her heel so her back wasn't to him. She crossed her arms. "I presume I will be staying in this room. I mean, you wouldn't have gone to all this trouble just to move me after a day, right?"

"I figured it would be easier to go ahead and place you in the queen's quarters, yes." Taiyo gestured to a door on the other side of the room. She'd tried it her first night but it had been locked. "That door leads to my quarters."

Hellebore moved toward her dresser, away from the door. She kept her gaze on the pins in her hand as she dropped them onto the wood. "Good to know."

She could feel the weight of Taiyo's gaze on her. If he wasn't going to say anything, what was he still doing there?

"Do you—"

"Should we discuss our terms?" Hellebore cut him off the second he took a step toward her.

He froze. "Our terms?"

"I used the right word, right?" Hellebore grabbed the dictionary and flipped through it, holding it to her chest. She looked up. "Rules? If I'm going to help you, maybe we should have some rules. If we're not to be at odds anymore."

Taiyo nodded, shifting back, clasping his hands behind his back and clearing his throat. "Yes… Yes, some rules might make this process a little smoother."

Hellebore leaned back against her dresser. "It might go without saying at this point, but just to be clear, since you only married me for my alchemy, that's *all* you'll be getting from me. That's all you really wanted anyway."

Taiyo started pacing, gaze on the floor. "Yes, of course."

Honestly, that was really the only rule Hellebore could think of.

His head snapped up. "I hope you know—I mean, I understand you don't have a favorable impression of me, considering I've strongarmed you into this marriage, but now that you know what it was for… I hope that you'll trust me. I would never force you into anything."

She raised an eyebrow.

He sighed. "Anything that wasn't strictly necessary to save my people."

"I trust you won't. Less because of any honor I think you have, but because you've already made it very clear this was a mercenary arrangement for you. And why wouldn't you? You think of me as a monster and a necessary evil. You're young. After I die, you'll have plenty of time to have a real marriage and everything that entails. You just have to be patient. Or poison me after I save your people."

But Taiyo wasn't laughing along with her.

He stopped in his tracks. "I would never do such a thing."

"It was a joke. And even so, to be fair, Your Majesty, I don't even know you. I don't know what you might do to me once my usefulness runs out."

Taiyo stared at the ground. Hellebore had no idea what he was thinking; she pushed off the dresser and took a step closer.

His head snapped up. "As for you, you won't cause any trouble? Your cooperation isn't some elaborate ruse and you have no intentions of following through? How can I be certain I can trust you?"

Hellebore gestured to her room. "This was an awful lot of trouble to go to if you aren't even certain you can trust me to do the one thing you brought me here for."

"That doesn't answer my question."

Hellebore grabbed the letter from her father on her nightstand and held it out to him. When he didn't immediately take it, she rustled the pages until he did.

Taiyo kept one eye on her even as he read.

She said, "What would be the point? I can't go back to Chymes, and if I'm going to be stuck here, I'm not so stubborn and prideful that I would sabotage myself in the process. Getting any kind of revenge on you does me no good. Even if I wanted it."

Taiyo's expression shifted as he looked up from the letter. "Do you?"

"I want to be a King's Alchemist. Give me that and I'll have no reason to want revenge."

He folded up the letter and passed it back to her, the discomfort that had overtaken him while reading it still lingering in his eyes. "I want to trust you."

"But you don't." Hellebore set the letter back down and

took a closer look at him. "And yet, you don't have a choice in the matter. You have to."

Taiyo moved to take a seat on a chair, the same one he'd sat in the day before. "I do."

Hellebore took her seat on the sofa across from him. "Clearly, that's not an easy task. I know, elves have longer memories, but you don't really have any other option. You can't hold the actions of others against me if you want me to save your kingdom."

Taiyo's eyes narrowed. "Elves know the nature of alchemists. Of your family."

Wait...

"Is this about my aunt? I don't know what happened when the two of you met twenty-five years ago. I mean, I know my aunt doesn't like you, but she never said why. Surely you can let go of that if my father was able to and was still willing to negotiate with you."

Taiyo took a deep breath. "Your aunt and I did not get along, and that's all that needs to be said on the matter. There will be no prying into the past. You are correct, though, I have been looking at you and seeing her, and that's not fair to you. We will add that to the rules. I can't promise to do it perfectly, but I will do my best not to hold the bad blood between your family and mine against you."

"Thank you. And as a gesture of good faith, I'll add that I won't hold you forcing this whole marriage against you." At the shock in his eyes, she added, "I'm going to at least try. The whole affair was instigated by you, but as you saw in my father's letter, he was looking for an excuse to oust me, so if it hadn't been you, it could have been someone else."

Taiyo looked down at his hands again, letting his hair fall into his face to hide his expression. Although Hellebore wasn't sure why.

When he looked up, there was a strange glint in his eyes. "Thank you. You don't know how grateful I am."

Hellebore didn't like the way he was looking at her, sitting so close their knees were brushing on their wedding night. They'd just established where they stood on that matter, so she knew it couldn't mean what she feared it meant, but just to be safe, she pushed herself out of her seat and headed for her wardrobe.

"Well, I think we've laid down some great rules to start with. Unless there's anything else you think I need to know before the morning, we should both get some sleep—" Hellebore was opening the wardrobe door, hoping to be able to tell the nightgowns from the day dresses, when a hand brushing the small of her back had her slamming into the wardrobe as she whipped around.

Taiyo shifted back, lifting his hands up in a harmless gesture. "Sorry, I didn't mean to startle you. I just... Do you need any help before I go?"

She'd sooner cut the dress off her than let him help her out of it.

She flashed him a grin. "I am so glad you asked." She then abandoned the wardrobe, ducking under his arm and reaching the glowing iris by her window. She gestured to it and said, "Your note didn't give me any information about the typical care for these. Given the predicament we're in, it's crucial to keep this one in good health. I'm sure you agree."

"I would have thought someone like you already knew everything you needed to about them." Taiyo lowered his hands, nodding. "Thanks to their magic, they're usually resilient organisms. You already have it in a good spot. There's no such thing as too much sunlight for them. Water it once in the morning. I'll have one of your maids bring you a cup the right size, and just do one of those when you wake up."

Hellebore nodded, reaching over to brush her fingers over the petals. "I'm not sure what my father claimed I was to you, but if he tried to say I was a great lover of plants and you took that to mean a gardener, you would be wrong. My studies were always focused on killing plants more so than keeping them alive."

"That's what you meant?" Taiyo's eyes narrowed. "You like to rot plants from the inside out?"

"Lucky you." Hellebore grinned before she turned back to the iris, admiring the soft glow. "Don't worry, I'll take care of this one. It will be good to have it for my work. Who knows how useful it could be?"

She was too absorbed in examining which part of the petals' intricate design the light was emanating from to stop the hand from grabbing her wrist. She gasped as she was ripped away from the plant. Her back hit one of the bedposts as Taiyo backed her up against the wall, hand tight around her wrist. She hissed as his fingers tightened, her still raw skin hidden beneath the sleeves and bandages.

His eyes burned as he hissed, "Not on your life, alchemist."

Hellebore tried to find a way to escape, but he had her cornered, one of her arms pinned against the stone while his other blocked her in. She sputtered, "Taiyo—"

"Swear to me. Swear on your life, alchemist, you will leave that iris out of this."

She had no idea what was going on. Why this had been the thing that had caused him to snap. But if that's what he wanted—

"I swear! Taiyo, I swear I won't use that iris for anything. I won't hurt it. I won't touch it other than to water it."

Taiyo stared down at her. His chest was heaving with labored breaths. Her own heart was racing under the weight of his examination. Finally, he seemed satisfied with her sincerity and his grip loosened.

He pulled back. His voice was frigid once again as he said, "See that you do. You might be an alchemist by birth, but you are a Sun Elf's wife. The Sunrise Iris is sacred to a marriage. To deliberately harm it or neglect, or worse, has the same severity as if you were to be found in another man's bed or if I were to raise a hand against you."

Hellebore pushed up her sleeve, looking down to examine her wrist to see if the cracked skin had started bleeding. His eyes followed the motion, but she was too busy checking the damage to care if he felt any guilt or not. She muttered, "Then it's a good thing this isn't a real marriage."

Thankfully there was no additional damage. It throbbed a little more than before, but it would ease soon enough.

Hellebore looked up, mouth open to tell him as much, but he was already across the room, disappearing through the door connecting their rooms. The door shut, and she was alone.

Hellebore dropped her wrist and glared at the iris beside her, mocking her with its glow.

She might be helping Taiyo save his kingdom, but that didn't mean they were on the same side.

It didn't matter. All that mattered was the alchemy.

CHAPTER 11

Now that Hellebore was nothing but a queen and wife in name, neither she nor Taiyo wasted any time. The next morning, she was up bright and early to her maids coming into her room, both warily eyeing the belt and outfit they were carrying for her. Although, when Elaine saw the mess Hellebore had made of her wedding dress, she was distraught over the shredded fabric.

Turns out cutting herself out of it hadn't been that hard given it had only been half completed in the first place.

Also, good to know the Sun Elves were less reserved than the other elves.

Hellebore wasn't prone to fits of elation, but she couldn't stop her savage grin as she took her things from Phoebe. As soon as she was back in her clothes and not draped in Sun Elf colors and styles, she breathed a sigh of relief. An alchemist once again.

Her mask and goggles hung around her neck as she fastened her belt around her waist and hitched her skirt accordingly so it was modest without getting in her way, leaving her boots showing and the elf maidens looking absolutely scandalized.

That was when the connecting door creaked open and Taiyo hovered in the doorway, with only a loose pair of trousers on, causing her maids to startle before quickly averting their eyes. She just grinned at him and said, "See? Now you've got your alchemist. This suits me much better."

He crossed his arms, dark circles under his eyes. "I have a few important matters to attend to, including seeing the Star Elves off. Phoebe and Elaine will take you to a space I've set aside that should be suitable for your work. It's already equipped with the best that we have. I expect your things will arrive in a few days; it shouldn't have taken them long to gather them from the academy and send them. I anticipate it will include equipment from your people, and should there be anything missing that you require, we will send for it after. Until then, organize your lab, review the work that I've had compiled, and at noon we'll go to the garden."

Being given such clear and unquestionable orders didn't grate against her skin. Not now that she was his alchemist.

Phoebe and Elaine led Hellebore to her new lab, and it was about what she expected—not the worst setup to exist, but clearly the Sun Elves weren't equipped for the kind of work she would be doing. She spent the morning reading over the work of King Taiyo's previous experts while she directed Phoebe and Elaine in setting up what she did have and organizing so there would be plenty of empty places for her incoming equipment.

She hoped Taiyo was right about her things including equipment. If Callahan had been in charge of gathering it, she couldn't be certain she'd be getting anything that would help her.

When Taiyo appeared again, this time at the lab door, he looked less tired, likely thanks to the sun's apex. He was also far more dressed, and she left behind her maids but not a plethora of vials. The glass tubes clinked softly in their pouch with each step as she followed Taiyo, who stayed quiet.

Before they reached the rotting garden, she pulled her goggles down and her mask up before looking up at Taiyo. "We ought to get you some too, if you're going to be the one to come with me every time I collect samples. While I haven't proven it yet, I'd be willing to place good money on the chances this can't be good for you to breathe in unfiltered either."

"Worried about me, alchemist?" He laughed. "Someone might think you actually have a heart."

Fine. If he wanted to breathe in poison, he could. If he did keel over, she'd be free from even being his wife in name too. Surely if he died and it was his own stubborn fault, her father would let her return to Chymes since she'd done all he'd asked.

Princess Haruko certainly wouldn't want to keep Hellebore if that happened.

"Didn't anyone tell you?" Hellebore asked as she turned around and walked backward into the rotting garden, smirking beneath her mask as it muffled her voice. "It should be arriving with the rest of my things. I was going to put its jar by the iris. They'll look great together."

His horrified and disgusted expression had her laughing as she pulled her leather gloves on and knelt into the decay.

She brushed her fingertips over the dark, browning petals. She then reached into one of her pouches and pulled out her snips and tweezers, cutting off what she needed before carefully depositing it into her vial.

She quickly collected her first round of samples, sticking to the worst of the rot for this round.

The whole time, Taiyo did nothing but hover at the entrance and stare at her. She was certain she was a strange, uncomfortable sight for him, but once she had what she needed, they departed.

As he escorted her back to her lab, she made a mental note that she needed to set up a sanitization system for leaving the garden and for her lab if she ever potted and brought any of the plants in there.

But for now, she just sent her maids to fetch her something to wear and she discarded the tainted clothes into a corner and slipped into the plain pink day dress they brought her as she went about her work.

She quickly fell into a routine, and by routine, she meant she quickly threw herself into the project, spending all her hours in her lab, breaking only for meals and sleep, seeing Taiyo in passing in the mornings and evenings, when she told him it was too early for her to be able to tell him anything. She didn't let herself think about the academy, Emerson, Callahan, or Palladia.

That was much easier said than done. During the day, she was completely focused on the rot, reading up on everything the Sun Elves had tried to save the irises as well as the description of the rot that had been slowly taking over their land over the last two decades. At night, however, she was stuck staring at the ceiling, ignoring the soft glow of the iris she begrudgingly watered every morning even though it had no use to her. That was when her memories wouldn't leave her alone.

One day, maybe Callahan's lack of faith in her abilities wouldn't hurt as much. But she didn't believe the sharp thorn in her side from not being able to say goodbye to her aunt and brother would ever go away.

At night was the only time she let herself feel. When the sun came up, the moon and her weakness disappeared, and she was empty of everything but alchemy.

Her things arrived a week into her marriage, and she left her lab early in the afternoon when she was intercepted with the news. Better to get everything organized so she could move forward with studying her samples first thing in the morning with superior equipment.

She opened the door to her room to see Taiyo already there, surrounded by her trunks and crates and bags. He had one crate open and was examining the chemicals contained in the glass.

He looked up from the vivid blue liquid as she shut the door.

"Looking for my heart?" Hellebore asked with a grin.

He sniffed. "I wouldn't put it past your people to have managed the feat."

"Unfortunately, it's still right here," Hellebore said, pressing her hand over it as she came farther into her room. She moved to open one of the trunks, looking over her shoulder at him as she said, "The organ at least. All it does is pump blood. There's nothing more to it."

Taiyo huffed, setting the container back in its place before coming up to her shoulder and glancing down at the trunk she had open to see it was full of her clothes. Now she would never have to wear a Sun Elf dress again.

She'd accidentally ruined two already while working on this project.

He looked at her plain blouses and skirts the way his sister looked at Hellebore.

She asked, "Would you rather I ruin all that fine silk or the dresses covered with painstakingly beautiful embroidery that must have taken so much work to artfully create while I'm up to my elbows in plant decay?"

He just glared at the second pair of gloves in the trunk, a gift from her aunt for her sixteenth birthday, identical to her aunt's own favorite pair. Her aunt had wanted Hellebore to have a pair with all her favorite formulas for transmutation. Just looking at the gloves threatened to bring back that pathetic homesickness that had been plaguing her, so she rustled through her clothes, nonchalantly throwing a blouse on top of them as she pulled out a skirt.

As soon as the gloves were out of sight, Taiyo straightened up and started looking about the rest of her things.

Her so-called husband was a foreign creature to her. Maybe once she'd solved the problem of the decay, she'd make him her next subject of study.

The next week, when she needed a new batch of samples, Taiyo came to escort her at noon like before, and when she opened the door, he immediately raised an eyebrow and stared at the bucket in her hand.

"Dare I ask?"

Hellebore just brushed past him. The water in it weighed a substantial amount, and she had no desire to stand around with it. "You'll see."

Then he took it from her, rolling his eyes and setting off without a word.

She didn't know what to make of it. Or him. It was a little late to play the gentleman.

But Hellebore also wasn't particularly desperate to lug it around, so she stayed quiet.

When they arrived, she had him set the bucket beside the door before they went into the garden again.

This time, instead of hovering by the entrance, he followed her through the garden, watching her more closely as she took both the worst rotted irises and some of the medium rotted.

As she carefully snipped petals, leaves, and stems for

her study, she looked up at him out of the corner of her eye and said, "Your reports from your past experts don't say anything about the origin, nothing about the enemy you mentioned. I know you said it started here, but someone brought it in here from somewhere else. Having the country of origin of the rot would go a long way in helping me. The solution could be tied to the source."

Taiyo scowled. "I... I don't know where they brought it in from. An enemy I should have known better than to trust got in here and introduced the disease in order to weaken us."

Hellebore clicked her tongue as she corked a vial. "Well, as a strategy, I unfortunately have to give the Moon Elves credit. They were playing a long gambit, and if not for me, it would succeed. I'll look into what they could have brought with them to cause this."

Now that she'd had a fair number of hours examining the rotting irises, there was something about it that was familiar. Unfortunately, that by itself didn't mean much. Decay was her area of study. If she couldn't figure out *why* it was familiar, then that sense was of no use.

"Can you do it in six months?"

Hellebore looked around at the garden, then up at the sun. Her breathing came out distorted and heavy through her mask. "There's no other option."

When they were finished, both covered in the filth, Taiyo shut the door to the garden behind them. "What was the bucket for? You didn't use it."

Hellebore pulled a piece of chalk out of her belt and started writing on the wall. Taiyo let out a shocked gasp, and he started to lunge for her.

In hindsight, maybe she should have just told him.

Because as she pushed her power into the transmutation, she slammed into the wall while the disinfecting mist scoured over them.

The mist faded and she could feel Taiyo pressed against her, the chalk having clattered to the ground as his hands pinned hers against the stone. She stared up at him, and his fury shifted into confusion as he stared down at her.

She let out a slight chuckle, highly aware that she was at his mercy. "Paranoid much? Or are you just always looking for excuses to get your hands on me?"

Taiyo, however, only narrowed his eyes. "What did you do?"

"I disinfected our clothes so we don't track toxin and rot back through your castle." Hellebore tried to nudge his leg, but really only succeeded in bringing them closer. She hoped the heat she was feeling flooding her cheeks wasn't visible. She should have left her mask up. "You're welcome."

He stared down at her, his breathing still heavy, not pulling back. This was as close as they'd been since their wedding night.

"Considering my whole purpose here is for alchemy, I assumed you already knew not every use of it is an attack."

"Right," he whispered, but he didn't let go or move back. Did he feel this was necessary? Was he really so afraid of what she could do that he needed this to feel safe?

"I did use it to save your life with the sedative, remember?"

Taiyo's eyes drifted down from her eyes.

She took a short breath. "If I wanted you dead, you'd be dead."

He started to shift even closer, and she didn't even know how that was possible, but then he pulled back slightly, finally loosening his grip on her hands, pinned against the stone.

At least he wasn't completely flush against her anymore, but he was still far closer than he should be if he was so rightly repulsed by her. He whispered, "Why did you agree to help me? Why not kill me and let my country rot?"

"I have a fascination with decay." Hellebore didn't pull her hands out of his grip. If this was what he needed in order to trust her, she'd let him have it. "And you read my father's letter. I don't have much of a choice. I like living. Being alive is an important element in being an alchemist. Skilled as we are, we haven't conquered death yet."

"Witty indifference will get you nowhere. You agreed to help me instantly. You were hysterical with elation over it. You could easily claim to help and do nothing and not a single elf here would be able to know if you were truly failing or faking. Tell me the truth."

He had her cornered. Literally.

"If you insist... Maybe it was just desperation from you, but you believe I'm capable of this. I'd like to prove you right."

"That's all it takes to soften your steel, mechanical heart? A little bit of faith?"

She grinned, pushing off the wall slightly and flush against him. "Look all you like, but I warned you. The heart's just an organ, and if it wasn't, I'd have it in a jar where it can do me no harm."

Taiyo's breath stuttered, brushing her cheek as he whispered, "You... I cannot comprehend what you are."

"Now, don't flatter me too much. My ego is already inflated enough from you needing my help." She tilted her head, his sunlight weaving between them. "I hope in the decades and centuries after me you tell everyone I was beyond your comprehension, your alchemist."

"I can promise you now, that will not happen."

"We'll see about that."

CHAPTER 12

Apparently, Hellebore's husband wasn't content to let her remain beyond his comprehension.

At least, Hellebore could think of no other reason as to why the next day Phoebe delivered a note to her from Taiyo, asking if she would join him for dinner.

Hellebore supposed a change of scenery might do her good, and it could be entertaining. Hopefully she'd escape this encounter without being cornered up against something.

She arrived in a small private dining room, not having bothered to change out of her Chymesian clothes. They'd fared well enough that day in the lab, and whatever Taiyo was hoping to get out of this, she would not let him forget what she was.

Taiyo sat at the head of the table as she walked in, rising from his seat to greet her with a respectful nod. She took the only other seat with a table setting, the one directly beside him, and asked, "What is this about?"

"Even alchemists eat, don't you?" Taiyo took his seat again and the servants began filling their glasses.

Hellebore stamped down the instinct to smile at his quip. "Not with elves."

"Then why did you accept?" Taiyo took a sip from his glass, but she could see the faint curve to his lips.

"If I answer that, I spoil your fun." Hellebore picked up her utensils and began cutting the venison on her plate.

Taiyo shifted back in his seat, moving for his own dinner, but keeping one eye on Hellebore. "How was your work today? Any progress worth noting?"

Hellebore easily fell into her role as the King's Alchemist, updating him on the project. She had to slow down more than usual, but thankfully her Iubian had improved substantially since her arrival. The daily practice and full immersion were smoothing out the rough edges and had made it easy to recall her old studies in the subject. She still wasn't as natural at it as a native speaker. That combined with the fact that she had to explain to Taiyo her reasoning behind why she was pursuing certain lines of examination and what exactly the techniques were since he had no background in the fundamentals of alchemy like a Chymesian king would made the debriefing slower than usual.

Taiyo asked a lot of questions. Not in any hostile or demeaning way, but there was a hesitancy in them. She didn't hold it against him. It was natural that even if he needed alchemy, he wasn't very comfortable with it. Still, he was making an effort. She hadn't expected that.

As dinner came to a close, he asked, "How is the iris?"

She set her empty glass back down after finishing it off. "Watered, enjoying the sunlight, and perfectly healthy. I haven't poisoned it... yet."

She braced herself for an outburst, but it never came. Taiyo just shook his head, leaning his chin into his palm, letting it cover his mouth, but there was a light in his eyes that reassured Hellebore she hadn't overstepped with her joke.

After that first dinner, every few days she would receive an invitation from Taiyo to join him again. When she asked what his reasoning for continuing to invite her again and again, he replied, "Honestly, while I know it's necessary for me to engage with my court and be seen, it's exhausting."

"If you wanted a companion for dinner who isn't exhausting, you shouldn't have chosen me. All I do is bring you more work to discuss."

"You're not exhausting. Not to me." Taiyo smiled. "Besides, it's important work. Your dedication is commendable and your passion enviable. I don't know if I've ever cared about anything the way you care about alchemy."

She narrowed her eyes at him.

"Wait, let me guess—care is too emotional a word for you, sunshine?"

Hellebore choked on the sip she'd been taking. She lurched forward to set the glass down as she coughed. A chair screeched and a warm hand was on her back as she pressed her napkin to her mouth while her body convulsed with a few more coughs. She looked over her shoulder to see Taiyo crouching beside her, having abandoned his chair.

"Are you alright?"

"Sunshine?"

Taiyo grinned, hand still on her back, only now it moved up and down, and Hellebore's heart kept racing. "What? You don't think it fits?"

Hellebore shoved at his shoulder, knocking him off balance, and he fell back against his chair with a laugh. "I see why you keep doing this. It's not your court that's insufferable. It's you."

The servants attending them exchanged a few glances, but none of them stepped in.

"Oh, you wound me so." Taiyo clasped a hand to his heart. His fingers curled into the fabric of his shirt as he grabbed the chair with his other hand and stumbled back to his feet. Hellebore glanced at his glass. He'd only had one, so he couldn't be drunk.

"Just sit back down and tell me what exactly this thing is so I can be certain you're not secretly trying to poison me." Hellebore pointed to the foreign vegetable on her plate she had not yet touched.

Taiyo sank into his chair before pulling it back up, closer to her side than before. "Don't worry, I ensured everything you're fed is safe for you to consume. Unlike some, I'm not in the business of accidentally poisoning people."

"If you don't let it go, the next one won't be an accident."

"Believe me, sunshine, you're not going to be the thing that kills me."

She stabbed at her food. Obviously. Elves and their ridiculous lifespans.

* * *

A month and a half into her research, Hellebore came back to her room, having long since dismissed Phoebe and Elaine for the evening. Taiyo hadn't extended her an invitation to eat with him, so she decided to press on with her work. She'd been deep in her experiment that involved the rotting irises and samples of the other plants being affected by the rot as well and needed to get her observations recorded, specifically for the request she was about to make.

But when she entered her room, she spotted a little bit of light underneath the door connecting her room to Taiyo's. So he was still awake. She started for the door, but the sound of voices on the other side stopped her from opening it.

"—nity! Don't be foolish."

Princess Haruko.

"She's been here over a month now and has done nothing but what she said she would. She's different, granted it may not be by much, but enough."

"You've thought that before."

Were they talking about the last time Taiyo had had any significant interactions with an alchemist?

"Yes, and I learned my lesson, but this time I have nothing left to lose."

Was it more than just a poor first impression with Aunt Palladia?

What more weren't they telling her? Did it have anything to do with her solving the rot? How could they expect her to solve the problem if they didn't give her all the information?

Their voices lowered and Hellebore had to strain to hear anything, and even then she couldn't make anything more out.

Then, Haruko said, "Please, don't look for something that's not there. She's a tool to be used. Nothing more."

Taiyo said nothing in response. Another door opened and shut. Hellebore waited approximately five seconds before she flung the door connecting their rooms open.

Taiyo jumped from his spot on his bed, catching himself on one of the four posts, eyes widening, skin paling, and face falling as he looked at her.

"Hellebore—"

But she was looking at the bottles on his nightstand beside the bed, stepping into his room for the first time. Interesting. What were they for? She waved her hand dismissively. "Don't worry. I'm not about to start screaming and throwing things at you."

"How long were you there?" Taiyo asked, still gripping the post so tightly his knuckles looked ready to fracture.

She breezed right past him, picking up the first bottle and looking over her shoulder. "Not long. I learned nothing new other than the fact that there's something you're not telling me. I already know you're desperate and that you arranged this marriage for the sole purpose of using me as a tool."

"My sister—"

"Doesn't like me. I know." Hellebore looked down at the bottle and peered at the liquid, identifying the substance within a second. "Painkiller?"

"Supposedly," Taiyo scoffed.

"Not doing much for you? Is this related to the thing your sister doesn't want you to tell me?"

He stared at her for a moment. "No. I get migraines. Always have. It's supposed to help so I can sleep. It doesn't always."

Hellebore turned it over and examined it more closely, then let out a little hum before tossing it to him and he scrambled to catch it. "Well, since you refuse to believe me when I've repeatedly told you I was trying to sedate you, not poison you, there's your proof. That tincture when combined with the sedative I used is lethal."

He stared down at it for a moment. He gritted his teeth and shook his head before staring at her. "Why are you like this?"

Hellebore raised an eyebrow. "If someone thought you purposefully poisoned them, wouldn't you point out it had been unintentional once you had more proof?"

"Not this." He took a step toward her, holding up the

bottle. He gestured at her, frustration seeping into his voice. "*This.*"

He came to a stop directly in front of her, cornering her against the bed and the nightstand. Here they went again. But all she did was stare at him with a cold, unbothered expression. She said, "Alchemy doesn't extend to reading minds. As brilliant as I am, not even I can do that. I'll need you to be more specific."

He reached around her, bracing his hand against the post, his arm hovering by her head as he leaned down. "Why are you so unfazed? Why does nothing bother you?"

"Can I have a few examples?"

"After thinking you were being kidnapped, only to discover it was actually because we were betrothed, you immediately acquiesced."

"You made it clear my refusal didn't matter, and given the circumstances, I see why."

"That's not the point. You just overheard my sister and me discuss something we haven't told you, but instead of being angry your husband is still keeping secrets from you, you're more concerned with my medicine?"

"Why would I be angry? It's not like our marriage is anything more than an arrangement. Why would I have any expectation of you divulging all your secrets? Besides, if it's relevant to my work in helping you and your people, the only people you hurt by keeping it a secret are you and your people. If you keep something from me that will help save your people, that's on your head, not mine. I have no stake in this. And if it's not relevant to my work, you have no obligation to tell me."

"If the Moon Elves attack during the eclipse, you'll need to care."

"I promise you that you don't have to worry your pretty

little head about me. I'll be able to protect myself and escape just fine."

"Really? Then how did I manage to abduct you and carry you off?" Taiyo smirked.

Hellebore narrowed her eyes. "Because I stopped to save you instead of letting you die in order to escape."

Taiyo shifted closer, chest brushing against hers. "And why would you have any desire to save my life?"

"Don't flatter yourself. I was just trying to avoid starting a war when I escaped. It had nothing to do with you."

"So pragmatic."

"Thank you."

He tilted his head. "My sister just called you a tool to be used. Aren't you offended? Why aren't you angry?"

"What use is there in being offended by such a fact? It does not make it any less correct. Emotions cannot prevail against truth." She lifted her chin, the action causing a few strands to come loose from her braid. "And why should it concern you, my lack of concern? I am your tool to be used. That's what a King's Alchemist is. And that is what I am to you. That is all I am to you."

"How did you open yourself up and piece by piece remove all your emotions one by one until there was nothing left but this cold shell?" His other hand came up to her cheek, brushing a loose strand back behind her ear. He whispered, "Where have you hidden your heart, sunshine?"

Her own voice came out as a whisper. "The heart is just an organ."

"And you're everything I feared you would be."

"Now if that were true, would I be so willing to help you save your people?"

He pulled his hand away and stepped back, shaking his head. "Was there a reason you were at my door?"

Right.

"I need to send for a few things from the Royal Alchemists' Academy. I have research there that I believe will help me identify the rot. It's familiar to me, but I haven't been able to place it. It's imperative."

He frowned. "And the one who would be overseeing that would be Palladia?"

"Yes, this would mean sending a letter addressing her." Hellebore also wanted an excuse to write her aunt since she'd never actually gotten to say goodbye, and maybe when her things were sent, she'd receive a response explaining a few things. "I have no intention of saying what I want my research for. I have been studying rot and decay for a long time. There should be nothing suspicious about it."

Taiyo scoffed and started pacing, but the color still hadn't returned to his face. He didn't look perfectly steady on his feet. Since the medicine had been out, he probably still had that migraine.

He seemed to be weighing it though, instead of dismissing it out of hand. Maybe he was semi-intelligent. He went to all the trouble of getting her to do this, so he'd better listen to her when she told him what she needed.

"It would be only your research, correct? Nothing of your aunt's? No other books?"

Paranoia was not a good look for him. If the secret didn't have to do with the painkiller, then it was obviously about whatever had happened that had caused him and her aunt to hate each other.

"That was my intention. I can make it clear that's all I expect."

Taiyo nodded. "Alright. Send for it."

Hellebore said, "I'll have my letter first thing in the morning for you to approve."

She then started to turn for the door when a hand caught hers. She looked back at Taiyo.

"I'm sorry."

"What?"

Taiyo dropped her hand, pulling his back to rest at his side. "That you can't write without my approval. It's a horrifically invasive thing."

"It is, but you're not the one who would destroy any letter I might send without your seal. Was it your idea or my father's?"

Taiyo immediately lowered his gaze.

Oh. She took a deep breath. "Well... What's done is done. Logically, I understand the reasoning. You'd never even laid eyes on me. You didn't know if you could trust me. Frankly, given what I heard, you still don't. Having you read my letters is a measure of trust, that you know I'm not trying to run off."

Taiyo's head snapped up. "That doesn't make it right."

"So? You've proven you have no qualms doing whatever it takes to save your kingdom. Now you're worried about being righteous?"

"I..." Taiyo took a step toward her. "I've had a lot of qualms about this whole affair."

"And it's far too late for them now. You've made your decisions. Now we all live with them."

"I—" Taiyo cut himself off. His voice came out softer. "Do you want to write to someone else? Your brother, perhaps?"

Hellebore had been doing an excellent job not missing Callahan or wallowing in the truth of what her brother really thought of her as an alchemist. Focusing on her work and dealing with her strange elf husband were perfect distractions. If only one of those distractions wasn't trying to now push her toward the very subject she wanted nothing to do with anymore.

At her stony silence, Taiyo stepped forward, voice picking up speed. "I won't read it, if that's what you're afraid of. I'll sign the page before you write and give you my seal."

"It's just my communication with my aunt you want to monitor, then." She gave him a split second to object, and he stayed silent. "Well, your offer is appreciated, but unnecessary. I have nothing to say to my brother."

"And what if he had something to say to you?"

"Considering how long I've been here and haven't seen a single letter from him apologizing or attempting to explain himself, I doubt that."

Taiyo reached for her hand again. "Hellebore—"

She ripped it back. "I don't need your pity. My brother signed off on our marriage, and you should be grateful he did. If my brother's actions did not speak loud enough for him then his silence now has. He believes I'm not good enough to be his alchemist. Congratulations, that means I'm yours. I'm not going to waste my time on someone who doesn't have faith in my skills. I'm going to focus on the ones who do believe in me. You."

Taiyo's hand hovered in the space between them. His eyes were locked onto hers. The same question burned in his eyes and so much more. The sort of things Hellebore had no experience with and had no intention of dealing with.

So, she brushed off her skirt and started for the door. "And on that note, that means I should go to bed so I can resume my work in the morning and have that letter for you to approve of."

As she went back to her room, Taiyo's eyes burned a hole in her back. She paused in the doorway and looked back, nodding at the bottle. "By the way, if that's not working for you, and you actually want to sleep, let me know."

Taiyo whispered, his voice coming out rougher and more raw than before, "And why would you care about me sleeping?"

"Maybe I'm just trying to keep you guessing."

"Hellebore."

She sighed like he was physically dragging it out of her. "I'm your alchemist. That's what we do. Serve and take care of our kings. It's got nothing to do with you or me. I'm just doing what I've been raised to do."

"I'm your husband."

"Not in any way that matters. Goodnight."

The reason she'd taken no offense to his continued distrust in her and any message she might send to her aunt? Well...

Hellebore only had one night to figure out how she was going to encrypt her real message to Aunt Palladia right under Taiyo's nose.

Whatever had happened between them twenty-five years ago, Hellebore was going to find out.

CHAPTER 13

Three weeks after Taiyo had signed off on Hellebore's letter, not even a hint of suspicion there might be more to it than met the eye, she received a response.

Although, said response so far appeared to simply be the fulfillment of the surface level request Hellebore had made for a few pieces of equipment and her research at the academy. If Taiyo hadn't thrown her over his shoulder and run off with her, she could have had this material months ago to work with.

Hellebore reached her room, Elaine on her heels, to see the door open and Phoebe directing the male servants where to place the crates. Hellebore quickly took over, practically chasing the elves out of the room as soon as all the crates were delivered. All but the one who appeared in the doorframe as Phoebe and Elaine were shooed out.

"I didn't realize you'd collected this much research in your time at the academy," Taiyo said, leaning against the frame and eyeing the crates that were all packed full of her notebooks and textbooks.

Hellebore knelt beside the first crate and started pulling out the textbooks in it. She looked over her shoulder at him. "I stayed busy. Only some of this is my research into types of plant rot. I spent a few years focusing on creating a new formula to change the makeup of steel into something more malleable. I only succeeded in shortening the formula by a few letters, so better but not the true efficiency I wanted in order to make it easier to manipulate an opponent's weapon in combat."

What a waste of two years that project had been.

But Taiyo was staring at her with that strange look again, like she was a foreign beast he'd never seen before.

It sent a rush up her spine and a flare of heat to her cheeks, and she didn't like that. She turned back to the crates, but she saw no letter tucked amongst them. Had her aunt not realized Hellebore had also written in code?

She must have taken the letter at face value. Or Hellebore's father had forbidden Aunt Palladia from including any kind of response. Aunt Palladia usually didn't let her brother have much say over her actions, but this was uncharted territory for all of them. She might have withheld a response in order to protect Hellebore from incurring Taiyo's ire in case he was reading her mail before giving it to her.

"I... I need to get back to work. The Moon Elves have been spotted at our borders again, and while it's not new, it's still a massive headache to deal with them and their king. I'll see you tonight for dinner," Taiyo said, moving to shut the door. "Let me know if you come across anything significant."

She waved him off, already trying to sort through the mess whoever had packed the crates had made of her organizational system. Eventually, she finally found her most recent notebook containing a substantial amount of her work in rot.

Hellebore was still on the ground, leaning against the crates as she flipped through her drawings of her dying plants back at the academy. She was halfway through it when an envelope fell out of the pages.

She should have known better than to doubt her aunt.

Hellebore glanced around, but Taiyo was long gone.

Really, Hellebore hadn't asked for much. Hellebore wanted her aunt's version of the story of what had happened between them since Taiyo was in no hurry to tell her. Or Haruko was still convincing him not to tell her, if she was correct in assuming the conversation she'd overheard had to do with whatever had happened between him and her aunt.

Hellebore eagerly opened it up, but the handwriting wasn't her aunt's. It was more masculine, and Hellebore couldn't place it.

All it said was:

Hellebore,

Come to the northwest corridor four hours after sunset on the first of the month. You'll get your answers then.

Well, that was sufficiently ominous.

The first of the month was two days away. Which meant she had two days to decide what to do about the note.

One, show it to Taiyo and get his opinion. The problem with that one was she'd also have to decide if she would tell him the truth that she'd gone behind his back and included a secret message to her aunt prying into the past, or lie to him and act like there was no reason for her to expect such a note.

Two, keep it to herself and show up prepared for either her aunt—who had chosen to disguise her handwriting and not sign the note—or to meet whoever it was that thought he could give her answers and had gotten access to her things either in transit or in the castle.

Three, don't tell Taiyo about the note and don't show up to what could be a trap.

That night at dinner, she kept her mouth shut, only telling Taiyo it would take her time to go through her research and see if there were connections. When he asked if Palladia had written back, she'd simply said no.

The first of the month arrived, and as her maids fluttered around her in the morning, she stared at her belt, trying to decide what to equip herself with in the event she did decide to risk it and walk into a trap on the chance it was actually from her aunt.

The dusty, barely functioning organ in her chest constricted, and Hellebore nearly gasped. She instead took a deep breath and ignored it.

But as she worked in her lab that morning, it still didn't go away.

There was something deep, something aching in what was supposed to be a purely functional space.

And all of this pain just at the thought that by not going she was missing a chance to see or at least hear from Aunt Palladia.

Hellebore hadn't let herself feel anything since her wedding. She hadn't cried since then either, and she wasn't going to start now.

"What's wrong?"

Hellebore looked up at Taiyo as he sat beside her during dinner. He'd been inviting her to eat every other day since she'd sent a message to Palladia.

Admit to the elf she was married to—who she'd been working hard to convince she was an emotionless, impenetrable fortress—that she was homesick and missed her aunt like someone had actually carved her heart out of her chest?

She'd sooner swallow her tongue and never speak again.

"Just thinking about the samples I'll be examining tomorrow. I'll be testing a tincture that I don't believe will cure anything, but my hope is that it will slow the decay in the garden. If it does, then I can move forward with developing something that will reverse the rot."

It wasn't a complete lie. That was true, just not what she was thinking about.

Taiyo clearly didn't believe her. "That sounds like good news, but you look like a rain cloud."

"Thank you."

"That wasn't a compliment."

"Well, we can't all be rays of sunshine—and I'm not; so don't even think about calling me that. The rain comes eventually. Night always falls." Hellebore picked at the fruit on her plate before giving him a stern look. "Maybe I look so grave because I don't want you to get your hopes up. My tincture could fail, and then I've made no tangible progress. Maybe I'm just trying to protect you. People always let you down eventually."

"And because of that it's better not to have any hope at all? Not to try?" There was something in his voice she didn't like. It was far too personal for their strictly professional relationship.

"Obviously I believe in trying, otherwise I wouldn't be spending all my hours in this lab trying to help your people. But I'm going to be practical about it. Until the solution is tangible, I won't hope that I have the solution. That's all."

Taiyo shook his head. "I never knew a stone wall could take on the guise of a woman for so long and never crack."

"Thank you."

Taiyo looked ready to climb over the table and strangle her. She grinned.

Then he laughed.

And she never knew what to do when he laughed. She never understood why.

As desperate as she was to never let him find out, he was right. She was starting to crack.

She wanted answers. She wanted her aunt. Only one person in her family thought she was worth anything, and Hellebore hadn't even gotten to say goodbye.

So if it was a trap, she'd be prepared, but if it was her aunt...

She was a hypocrite. She hoped it was her aunt.

So instead of going back to her room after dinner like she usually did, she made an excuse to Taiyo that she had some more work to wrap up before going to bed. She went back to her lab to wait. Her belt was stocked full of anything she might need to ward off an attack. She twirled a thin knife in her fingers, typically used for dissection, but it had its purposes elsewhere. Alchemists didn't fight with typical daggers or swords anyway.

It was nearly pitch black when she left her lab and stepped out into the hallway. Moonlight came in through the windows on the other side of the hallway, giving her just enough to see by as she crept through the hallways and to the corridor. She was going half an hour early. If it was a trap, she'd be waiting with her own.

She reached the corridor, pulling out her chalk as she turned down the hallway, goggles resting on her crown and mask around her neck. She looked around and saw no one, so she moved to write her first formula. She was halfway through it when all the moonlight vanished, and all that was left was darkness.

So it was a trap. And they were already there, waiting for her.

She reached into her pouch and grabbed a smoke bomb, activating the prewritten formula and throwing it before pulling her mask up and stumbling to her feet.

She heard no coughing.

Who was it? Where were they?

She stumbled back, but the darkness was absolute. Their control of the moonlight and the time of night gave one distinct, likely possibility. Moon Elves.

But she heard no breathing, no footsteps, nothing.

If she ran, would she just run right into them?

Then the sound of glass breaking ripped through the air. Her smoke started to dissipate, and a sliver of moonlight came through, highlighting the gray smoke.

Two figures came through, and before they could attack her, she attacked first. She lunged forward, driving her knife toward where she estimated a Moon Elf's chest would be. She missed the elf, twisting, but she still threw her weight forward. It worked. He stumbled back with a gasping grunt and went right back out the window with a yell.

Then arms quickly went under and around her, preventing her from moving her arms. She jerked and coughed as smoke filtered through her mask before it was ripped off her face completely. Out of the corner of her eye and in the moonlight, she could see now she'd been correct. Their silver hair and markings gave them away, as did their clothes. Moon Elves. With masks on?

They were well prepared against an alchemist then.

The elf said something, but she couldn't make it out beneath his mask and her harsh coughing. Plus, she didn't know their dialect of Elvish anyway, so it wouldn't have mattered.

She wasn't getting kidnapped by elves a second time. Her pride couldn't stand it. So she went completely limp, holding her breath so she didn't give herself away.

As soon as she did, the elf dropped her and rushed to the broken window where she'd pushed his compatriot out of. This was her chance.

Except when she tried to get up, her arms weren't moving as fast as she was willing them to. Her feet weren't moving at all. She gasped and choked. A paralytic.

Had he injected it when he'd had her restrained?

Her smoke bomb hadn't had one. Although it would have been smart but useless since they had masks anyway.

But now she couldn't even move to escape. She couldn't even twitch her fingers, having only crawled a few feet down the hall by the time the second elf had helped the first back in through the window. They looked at her, but she couldn't make out anything beneath their goggles and masks. They exchanged a few more words, some sort of argument, but it was muffled. There was something about their voices or their words that was familiar, but she supposed their dialect was similar to Iubian Elvish. If she tried, she might be able to translate a few words.

Not that it helped her get out of this. She couldn't move her fingers. She couldn't transmute. She was utterly helpless and maybe if she was lucky, they would put her out of her misery and kill her now so she wouldn't have to live with the humiliation of being kidnapped twice by elves.

No wonder her father and brother had so quickly agreed to marry her off. She was worthless as an alchemist.

The two elves hurried toward her and one of them quickly slung her over his shoulder. The second moved to secure their escape, starting to climb out of the window first, a rope tied to a stone carving protruding from the castle wall.

What a disgrace she was. Unable to best even just two Moon Elves.

The one carrying her was about to climb out the window when blinding bright light ripped through the air. The elf reached for his eyes, crying out, and Hellebore could see nothing. She just squeezed her eyes shut, trying to protect herself from the agony.

"Get your filthy hands off my wife."

CHAPTER 14

Hellebore's vision cleared. The elf carrying her had caught himself on the window frame, not dropping her; his other hand remained curled around her legs.

Taiyo stood down the hall, the fading smoke curling around his legs as he held his arm out, more sunlight starting to gather at his fingertips.

"You won't live to see your next moonrise, but unhand her now and I will consider making it a quick death." Taiyo continued approaching, and the elf carrying her launched into action.

He pulled something out of a belt and threw it at Taiyo with an enraged yell.

It barely flashed in the sunlight and smoke, but Hellebore thought it looked like her knife. When had he picked it up? Unfortunately, Taiyo was too focused on the sunlight and fire to see it until it was too late. He tried to twist at the last second, and it cut through his shoulder. It didn't embed in his heart at least.

Hellebore could do nothing but watch.

Actually, she could do nothing but fall out of the window as she was thrown out it by the elf carrying her. She couldn't even scream.

Taiyo, however, could.

He screamed her name as the wind rushed around her and her death fast approached, except, she couldn't even see the ground.

She shut her eyes and cursed herself for every single failure and foolish, overconfident thought that had led her to plummeting to her death. But instead of slamming into the ground, arms wrapped around her, catching her for a brief second before they both hit the ground. She blinked to see it was the first elf, groaning at how her weight had just slammed him into the ground as well.

"Hellebore, shut your eyes!"

She immediately obeyed Taiyo's command and the Moon Elves were not so quick, given their screams and the thud she heard. She could see the bright flash from the inside of her eyelids and then she smelled something burning. The screaming increased, and she blinked her eyes open to see Taiyo had followed them down into the courtyard and had the closest one by the arm, one hand in his back. The Sun Elves didn't just command sunlight—with their light came heat and fire.

Taiyo had been serious. He was going to kill them.

The elf who had caught her realized it at the same moment as he shot to his feet and pulled out something from a pocket. Glass broke and all the light vanished again, leaving them engulfed in shadows.

Moon Elves were known for seeing much better at night than other elves and especially humans. Although what the goggles' purpose had been, Hellebore wasn't sure.

She heard Taiyo's voice again, a pained scream, and

then there was nothing but the sound of labored breathing through masks and darkness.

Then a hand grabbed her ankle and they started to pick her up. She couldn't get her mouth to fully open, but she managed an absolutely pathetic whine.

"Hellebore—" Taiyo's voice was strained, like he was talking through gritted teeth.

But then the elf trying to drag her hissed in pain and one of them said something. They had some kind of quick argument.

Then a hand grabbed hers and she was pulled away from the Moon Elves, and someone was crouching over her, one hand braced on the ground. Taiyo. It could only be him. His breathing was so much louder, but then he spoke.

"I'll give you five seconds before I blind you and burn your hearts out of your chests. Five."

The sound of footsteps filled the darkness as Taiyo counted down. As the Moon Elves got farther away, the darkness receded. Not by much, but the moonlight came back and the Moon Elves were gone as Taiyo breathed out, "One."

Now that she could see, she saw he was on his knees, one hand braced on the ground. His chest was above her head as he was using his whole body to shield her from being taken again. His other arm was wrapped around his stomach.

His hand was covered in black blood.

He was bleeding from the shoulder as well, but that was a shallow cut compared to the wound he was clutching. A little bit of the same black blood was coming up to the corner of his mouth.

He stared at the empty courtyard for a moment. Then down at her.

She was still paralyzed. She couldn't make any noise

other than a humiliating whimper in the back of her throat.

Then he dropped to the ground beside her, rolling over and throwing up on the stone away from her. Black blood.

Was it even blood?

He curled in on himself and his eyes started rolling into the back of his head all while she was screaming in hers.

He wouldn't dare. He wouldn't dare die and leave her like this.

She couldn't help him. All she could do was lie there, useless while he bled out beside her.

Then he was getting his arms underneath him, painfully slow, sweating as his hair stuck to his skin. He looked down at the stone before he got back to his knees, the moonlight framing him as his head tilted back to the sky. He grunted, grabbing his shirt and tearing it the rest of the way, fully exposing his wound. Then, to her shock, he took his hand, lighting it with a mix of sunlight and fire.

He was going to—

As soon as he pressed his palm to the wound, the burning smell returned and the noise he made was going to haunt Hellebore's nightmares. His face screwed up in agony would accompany it.

What was worse was when it was over, and his hand fell and he slumped slightly back down. Then he took his hand again and it lit with his magic, and he reached over, scorching the ground where his blood was so no one would ever see anything but the burn. He took several deep breaths, wiping his filthy blood-stained hands on his clothes before he came crawling back over to Hellebore, and his face filled her vision as he took her face in his hands.

"Hellebore, it's alright. You're safe. I've got you. You're going to be fine."

She just swallowed.

But he wasn't. Sun Elves bled red just like the rest of

them.

"Did they give you a paralytic?"

She was able to give the tiniest of nods. Which meant it was starting to wear off, but it was doing so slowly.

"Alright, I'm going to get you back to your room and then I'll call a healer."

How was he—

Taiyo was scooping her up and into his arms, staggering slightly as he stood up, but quickly regaining his balance and securing her in his arms, one arm under her knees and the other around her back. He adjusted his hold until she was comfortably tucked into his chest, her head resting against his shoulder.

But with no voice, Hellebore couldn't protest and insist he leave her on the ground to let it wear off or go find a healer for himself first. All she could do was let him slowly, carefully, like she was something precious to be handled delicately, carry her back inside the castle and through the hallways and to their rooms.

She hated it. She hated him.

As more feeling returned, her eyes welled up and she had no choice but to turn her head deeper into his shoulder to hide it.

"You're safe, sunshine," Taiyo murmured, somehow managing to shift her even closer. "I made a vow to protect you, and I have. I always will."

If she had her voice, she would have come up with something between a laugh and a sob and told him that those vows didn't mean anything.

Instead, feeling came back into her fingers, but not her arm. So she just curled her fingers into the tatters of his shirt.

She heard a door creak open, and she shifted her head just enough to see her room greeting them. Guilt turned her stomach at the sight of her crates of research that had contained the note for the trap she'd foolishly fallen for.

He quickly started toward her bed, but the last thing she wanted was to stare at the evidence of her duplicity. The word caught in her throat, not quite coming out as a word, but yet another displeased whine. Taiyo froze, glancing down at her.

"No?"

She nodded.

Taiyo just stared down at her with a dumbfounded expression, and she had no clue what was going through his head. But whatever it was, it worked in her favor since he headed for the door connecting their rooms. Once they were in his room, he quickly but gently set her down on his bed before moving back.

She couldn't stop him from slipping out of her grip even as she'd tried to hold onto his shirt.

"I'll—I'll be—" Taiyo started as he began to move for his door but quickly had to catch himself on one of the posts to keep himself from hitting the floor. He closed his eyes. "I'm—I'm fine. Just dizzy."

"H—He—Healer—" Hellebore managed to choke out. "Y—You."

He shook his head. "No. It's just for you. I'm going to be fine in a minute."

"W—Wear o—off."

He turned back and looked at her, something strange in his eyes.

She whispered, "Stay."

"You…" Taiyo turned around fully, an intensity to his gaze that would have frightened her if she hadn't just been nearly abducted. "You want me to stay?"

"Yes," she breathed out.

The last thing she wanted was to be alone, completely

helpless, even if the paralytic was wearing off.

Taiyo staggered back to the bed, climbing onto it in the space he'd left beside her. His bed was huge, so there was plenty of room for two people to lie side by side and not touch, as evidenced by them at that very moment.

They lay there exactly like that as the minutes stretched on. The only noise in the air was their breathing. Little by little, more feeling came back, but it was agonizingly slow and terrifying to be so vulnerable.

Hellebore didn't really know what possessed her to make such a request, but she had. It wasn't like she was much safer with him nearby when he looked two seconds away from death and was refusing to get a healer for himself.

It only meant one thing…

She turned her head, finally able to move her neck so that she faced him. He was lying on his side, facing her, eyes never having left her even when they were half lidded from exhaustion.

"You're dying. Aren't you?"

"Clever girl." His eyes opened wider. "What gave me away?"

"Healthy elves don't bleed black blood. But I should have put it together sooner."

Looking back now, it felt painfully obvious.

"Well, I'm not breathing my last tonight. I will tell you everything tomorrow."

"How did you find me?"

He sighed, burrowing his head into his pillow. "It was late. You hadn't come back. I was worried. Turns out I had good reason to be."

She could feel her calves. That was good. She shifted her feet.

His hand found hers, resting in the space between

them. His fingers skimmed over her palm, and when she shifted them in response, he laced his fingers through hers. "What happened?"

She closed her eyes but she didn't pull her hand away.

He'd accused her of being a stone wall incapable of cracking.

She wished he was right.

"I was foolish." Her voice broke.

Taiyo pushed himself up slightly, shifting slightly closer but not fully closing the gap between. "Tell me."

She closed her eyes. "You'll be angry."

"Not tonight. Tonight all I care about is the fact that you're safe. Tomorrow? I will still be glad I got there in time, and maybe I will be frustrated, but that will be tomorrow's problem."

She cracked one eye open. "There was a note among my research telling me to go."

She waited for his words to be false. She'd managed to find the end of his patience before, and if anything could provoke him to it again, it was this.

Instead...

"Why didn't you tell me? Why did you go?"

If he was angry, he was doing a good job hiding it because all she heard was plain confusion.

"Because... part of me... In my letter to my aunt, I hid a secret message. I asked her to tell me what happened when the two of you first met. So... I hoped it would be her."

She waited for the rage.

"I see."

Where was it? Why now was he being so patient with her?

"I was fairly certain it wasn't. I knew it could be a trap, and I thought I was clever enough to be able to get out of it anyway."

"I see."

Well, if he was angry, he was at least honorable enough to keep his word and save it all for the morning. Maybe she hadn't been giving him enough credit this whole time.

"But even when I went early to try to trap them, they were already expecting me."

"Why... Why didn't you tell me? Do... Do you really think so little of me?"

She couldn't stop the tears again. "And reveal to you how right you are to think as little of me as you already do? Show you that I'm not even the intelligent, capable alchemist you were after? Admit to you that I miss my aunt, that you despise, but she's the closest thing I've had to a mother for most of my life? That I'm pathetic and homesick and that I was so desperate for there to be anyone left in the world who cares about me that I walked right into a trap?"

She was sobbing now, burying her head into the sheets until she was being pulled up into Taiyo's arms as he leaned them against the headboard. He quickly undid her belt and tossed it to the side, then pulled her goggles and mask fully off her head and neck, throwing them to the side. Then he wrapped his arms around her, crushing her to himself, one hand curled around her waist and the other running up and down her back. Without her goggles and belt, she was able to sink into him, as much as she could as she was still fighting off some numbness but was mostly consumed with her sobs.

She curled her fingers into the back of his shirt when she managed to get her arms around him and buried her head against his chest. His heartbeat was almost sluggish in its loudness.

"I don't think little of you. I never would have married you if I did."

She hated how soft and warm she found his hands on her. She hated how much she wanted them to stay on her.

"And where would you ever get the idea one mistake makes you anything less than the most intelligent, capable, and dedicated alchemist? Do you think I would hold you in any less esteem because you miss having a mother? Do you truly believe there is no one who cares about you? Sunshine, look at me."

His hand left her back to gently tilt her jaw up to look at him through her watery eyes.

"Let me make myself clear. I care about you."

The word at the tip of her tongue was: why?

Why would he care about her? When he only knew her because he had been looking for a solution to his problem? Why care about anyone when he was dying?

But she said nothing in response.

His thumb brushed over her cheek. "And maybe one day you'll believe me."

She couldn't bear to look at his expression, overflowing with emotions that fascinated her and horrified her all at the same time. So she just buried her head in his shoulder and hated herself for the pained, resigned sigh she got in response.

At some point she started dozing off and that was when Taiyo shifted her back to her original place, pulling back completely.

Hellebore finally had her full mobility back. She let out a disgruntled huff and quickly grabbed Taiyo, holding him in place so she could move back into his arms, resting her head on his chest. His arm looped around her waist again.

Hellebore didn't want to examine why she would do such a thing.

Or why the strange, sluggish beat of his heart was a weight on her shoulders and a comfort all at the same time.

CHAPTER 15

Hellebore was perfectly content where she was, but where she was, however, was not perfectly content to let her stay that way.

She woke up, blearily blinking in the early dawn to see Taiyo pushing himself up and throwing one leg over to the other side of her so he was straddling her waist. She raised an eyebrow and said, "Dare I ask what you think you're doing?"

"I'm keeping my word." Taiyo sat back on his knees enough that he wasn't completely cornering her in. "It's morning. Now I get to be frustrated with you."

"And you can only do that hovering over me and looking down at me?"

Taiyo raised an eyebrow. "I'm making sure you don't bolt and almost get yourself captured again."

Hellebore huffed but made no protest or attempt to shove him away. She just gave him the cool, indifferent look that always had his eye twitching.

If he got to be frustrated, she got to be emotionless.

"You went behind my back."

"I did. And it was for nothing because my aunt didn't even reply to the message." And now Taiyo knew she'd been trying to pry into the past after they'd made it part of their rules not to.

"Not today, but soon, I will tell you what happened." He didn't even give her a chance to respond, breezing past it to continue, "More importantly, what concerns me most is that you knew it was likely a trap, but instead of thinking it through and trusting me, you only trusted yourself and didn't think of the consequences."

Hellebore gaped at him, processing his promise he would tell her and trying to catch up to what he'd just said. After opening and closing her mouth a few times, she started pushing herself up onto her elbows as she choked out, "I admit it. Yes, I was foolish."

"I don't think you realize what the real problem here is. You thought you could handle anything because you're a skilled alchemist. That's the only thing you were thinking."

And now she'd exposed the truth. Everyone else was right about her, and he knew now he was stuck with a mediocre alchemist at best.

"I overestimated my own abilities, I am aware," Hellebore said through gritted teeth, glaring up at him.

"No." Taiyo leaned in closer, his hair spilling over his shoulder and the orange ends brushing her cheek. "You *underestimated* your value."

His words slammed into her, nearly taking her arms out from under her. She shrank back slightly into the pillows helping prop her up, unable to make any sense of his words. How could he possibly think that?

"You still think of yourself as an alchemist exclusively. The fact that you are my wife, the queen, never crossed your mind. It never occurred to you that our enemies would take you because of your value to me and not because of your alchemy."

He was right. But did she admit it? She'd done an awful lot of admitting to him the night before.

She whispered, "Should it have?"

"You are my wife."

"Only so you could have an alchemist."

His gaze darkened, and he shifted lower. His fingertips brushed her cheek, moving to gently cradle her jaw. "You might be my alchemist, but you are my wife first. Not the other way around. Is that clear?"

A knock sounded on the door, saving Hellebore from questioning what he was trying to imply by that specific phrase. "Your Majesty, did Queen Hellebore leave already?"

Her maids.

"No," Taiyo called out, sitting back on his heels again, a smug grin on his face. "She's right here. Go ahead and draw her a bath and she'll be right in."

Heat flooded Hellebore's cheeks at the implication, and she quickly pushed herself up, glaring at Taiyo as her maids stammered an embarrassed assent from the other side of the door. Taiyo easily shifted back, letting her scramble off the bed.

She brushed off her clothes, but there was no use as they were filthy, and so were his. He was right, she did need a bath. She said, "While I will attempt to be more cognizant of my full position the way the rest of the world views me and I will promise to take more care and not go behind your back again, don't think that or last night changes anything on a fundamental level about this arrangement."

"A romantic, aren't you?"

Hellebore didn't dignify that with a response and

simply headed back to her room to clean up. He was just trying to get under her skin.

Her maids didn't look at her directly the whole morning, but Hellebore was the one blushing every time they looked away. It was ridiculous. Nothing had even happened, and even if it had, they were married.

As soon as she was dressed, as much as she could be with her belt, goggles, and mask on the floor of Taiyo's room, a healer was coming in on Taiyo's orders to look her over. Hellebore let the healer do his job, but she rolled her eyes the whole time. She was perfectly recovered. It had just been a little paralytic, nothing major.

What concerned her most was the fact that Taiyo was dying, and she still hadn't gotten answers about it. But when she finally got rid of the healer and tried to burst through his door since it was her turn to corner him, he was already heading through the other door, cleaned up, saying, "I have to go deal with the fact that two Moon Elves managed to get past our guards, into the palace, and find you without anyone seeing them. I'll see you tonight."

"Hypocrite!" Hellebore called out as his door shut behind him.

Fine.

She went about her day like usual. Only her "like usual" was plagued by a strange pit in her stomach as the leaves in her samples crumbled to black rot. When she looked at her vials of the petals suspended in liquid, she only saw Taiyo's thick, black blood on the stone.

When she dropped a beaker and the glass shattered, all she could do was stare at it, unable to feel her own fingers like the paralytic had returned.

She was here, playing with plants, while Taiyo was dying. She had a thousand questions, but what was most disconcerting to her was the fact that she was wondering... Was there a way to save him?

Why did she care if he died? Why would she want him to live?

CHAPTER 16

Hellebore left her lab right before sunset. She'd made no progress with Taiyo's slow death haunting her every step.

She had her maids help her change into a night-gown early so she could dismiss them, not paying any attention to their selection as she was focused wholly on the strange turning of her stomach and tightening of her chest when she wondered how long Taiyo had left.

She then went through the door connecting their rooms, but Taiyo wasn't back yet, so she settled for pacing while she ruminated.

He wanted to get onto *her* for going behind his back, not trusting him, not valuing her position?

She was ready for a fight when his door finally opened and he stepped into his room, face pallid, looking like he'd been run over by a carriage, and the fight in her eased. It didn't vanish completely, but it softened, not that she could ever let him know that.

What on earth was happening to her?

He looked up after shutting the door, startling to see

her. His eyes widened as they travelled over her standing in front of the window. A brilliant sunset was behind her, painting her in its light. But he wasn't looking at the sky. She looked down to take note of what she had on.

It was a silk nightgown that fell to her ankles and dipped lower in the neckline than her usual attire. Mostly because exposed skin was a hazard as an alchemist. However, the nightgown had a soft, sheer capelet falling around her shoulders and chest, the hem of it hovering below her bust, trimmed with a lace that shimmered in the light of the sunset coming in through the windows. The colors were different than her usual attire, certainly. The silk started at the neckline as a soft pink before it faded into a gold which faded into orange traveling down to her ankles. The capelet had a gold tint to the sheer fabric. She hadn't worn Sun Elf colors since her own clothes had arrived after the wedding.

She looked up to see Taiyo was staring at her. He took a deep breath, lips twitching up in a smile before starting to cross the distance between them. His voice was low and husky as he said, "Hellebore—"

The intense, heavy look he was giving her, along with the speed with which he was approaching, sent a jolt through her, causing her heart to race. She quickly stepped back, crossing her arms and saying, "I'm here for that explanation you owe me."

His step faltered, and he came to a stop beside the bed. His gaze darted over her again before slowly pulling back up to her face, and Taiyo's voice still sounded off as he said, "That's all you're here for? Nothing else?"

"I broke a beaker today. I haven't done that since I was thirteen."

At her abrupt non sequitur, he leaned back against the post, the look in his eyes fading as it was replaced with something softer. "Is it the paralytic? The healer said it was all gone and there were no side effects."

"No. It wasn't that." Hellebore huffed, rolling her eyes. "You don't get it. You don't understand *why* I dropped it. I got nowhere today. I haven't been able to focus on anything, and it's all *your* fault." Now that he wasn't looking at her so strangely, she regained her confidence and took a few steps toward him.

"How is it my fault?"

"Because all day there has been one thing and one thing only on my mind, driving me to distraction." Hellebore dropped her hands to her hips, voice rising as the frustration of the day caught up to her again.

Taiyo still stared at her dumbly.

She scoffed and pointed both hands at him. "You! All day, the only thoughts in my head are of you, and it is *maddening*. Because of you, I cannot focus. I cannot *think* of anything but you!"

But instead of being insulted at her fury-laced words, the look from before returned and he quickly pushed off the post, crossing the distance between them. A smirk spread across his lips and he laughed softly. "I don't see the problem here."

She didn't see what exactly these mood swings meant. Or maybe she just didn't want to deal with them. For an elf, he had so much emotion, it was overwhelming. Why couldn't he focus?

She put her hand out between them and stopped him in his tracks, pressing her palm to his chest where his sluggish heartbeat pressed against her fingertips. She narrowed her eyes. "This isn't amusing! You're dying, and all day I have been unable to escape that fact. I have been climbing up the walls, tormented by the image of you bleeding out, trying to understand what it is that's killing you. You promised to tell me, so tell me."

He stilled at her hand pressed against his chest, but he didn't pull back, just let her rest her hand over his heart. The intensity faded from his eyes once more. "You want to know what's killing me, sunshine? It's the same thing that's killing the irises."

"What?"

"I'm rotting from the inside out. That's why my blood is black." Taiyo reached up and wrapped his hand around her wrist, pressing her palm closer against his chest. "The rot hasn't been plaguing us for the last five years, or even the last ten. I've been taking on the rot threatening my country and people for years, using myself to slow the damage and decay and buy time to try to find a way to save the irises."

The sludge his blood had become... The pain he was clearly in every day... All to buy a little bit of time. She looked up from their hands and whispered, "How long do you have left?"

"The eclipse." His thumb brushed over her pulse, smooth and steady compared to his. He nodded toward the last few rays of the sun. "My magic is the only thing that has kept the rot from killing me already. When the eclipse occurs, all the Sun Elves will be without any connection to our magic, even me. If the Moon Elves attack, even without their magic, my people will all be fine afterwards as long as our defenses hold and you stop the rot from spreading further and save the irises for the future. Without my magic, I will be dead."

"That's why you came to us. You're out of time," Hellebore whispered.

Taiyo gave her a pained, bitter grin. "My apologies again, for how we got here, taking you even when I thought you were running away and forcing this on you, but now you see, I knew this would always be temporary for you. I wasn't condemning you to me for the rest of your life. Just the rest of mine."

"Wait, hold on," Hellebore said, mind spinning. "No matter what I do, you still die?"

He nodded, a strange peace in his eyes. "My blood is too far gone. My heart will be unable to handle pumping my blood in a few years even if the eclipse wasn't coming. My healers have already tried to use the healthy ones, when we still had them, and all it did was just infect them and destroy their magic. All I ask is for you to finish your work, and ensure the land is cleansed of the rot even if I die before you finish. I know I have no right to ask of you anything, but do you see now all I've done was out of desperation and a desire to do the least amount of damage?"

"Four months. I have a little under four months."

Hellebore ripped her hand off his chest and out of his hand as she started pacing, running a hand through her hair. "You couldn't have told me from the beginning? Now I only have four months!"

"I didn't know if I could trust you."

"Ugh. Right. Alchemist. Palladia's niece—whatever she did to make you think so poorly of her. Still, even with my head start on the rot affecting the plants, it would have been far better if I could have had more time to get started on this too. There's a massive difference between an elf's biological makeup and plants, so there's the strong possibility the cure for your blood is going to be different than the one for the plants—"

Hands grabbed her shoulders and turned her to face Taiyo again as he gaped at her. "What are you talking about?"

"Was I not clear?" Hellebore tilted her head. "There's nothing to be done for the loss of time now. So first thing in the morning I expect you to march yourself down to my lab so I can collect my first round of samples so that I can make up for the lost time. I've only got four months to save your life in addition to your whole country."

"You—You—Hellebore, I didn't marry you for you to save my life. The only reason I married you was because I knew that upon my death, you would be free." He was leaning down, much closer to her eye level than normal as his voice lowered. "I'm not asking you to save me."

"That's part of your problem. You didn't bother asking, which means I'm on a tight timeframe."

"No. You don't understand. Frankly—I don't understand. You're acting like you have to save my life. That couldn't be further from the truth. You have no obligation to me to do so. You should be relieved to hear that in a little under four months I'll be gone. You should want me to die. When I die, you get to go home, back to your people, your life."

The echo of what she'd accused him of was now haunting her.

And if she was being honest...

"I don't think of saving you as an obligation. The thought not to never occurred to me. Saving you was my instinct."

Taiyo straightened back up, taking a slow step backward, stumbling and falling to sit on the bed. His hands slid from her shoulders to her hands, accidentally pulling her a few steps with him as he landed on the mattress, now looking up at her.

The intensity in his eyes was so much stronger than what she'd seen at the start. This was so much fuller, so devastatingly full of emotion and something she couldn't name. And this frightened her even more than before. Emotions usually did.

But she didn't pull away. She just needed to be clear what this was about.

"Why?" Taiyo's whisper cracked on the word, hands clutching hers.

Why indeed?

She wondered what his answer would have been if she had managed to ask him the same the night before. But the moment was long gone, and that was for the best. His answer to such a question could only bring more agony to his already failing heart.

"I have no desire to go back to Chymes. I can't." She took a deep breath and stepped closer. "And they don't want me back. Even if the threat of treason wasn't over my head, returning after your death... If my brother truly wanted me to act as his King's Alchemist, he would never have agreed to the betrothal. If my father thought I was capable, he wouldn't have used me as a pawn to bargain with. They didn't know what you wanted with me, even if you were asking for their best. But they wanted an alliance and were happy to get rid of me."

"Hellebore. I didn't ask for their best. I demanded it." His grip on her hands tightened as his voice darkened. "I threatened your father with war if he would not give me your hand. They didn't want to send you away. I made them. Don't hold my actions against them. Your family—your brother, I'm certain he would give anything to have you back in his court and away from the Sun Elves who stole you away."

Hellebore's tightening throat was proving to be a problem, threatening to choke any word she might form. She took a deep breath. "I don't—You don't know that, and neither do I. My family's actions can speak for themselves, and the last thing you should be doing is arguing their case when doing so means letting you die!"

"That doesn't answer my question. If you don't want to go back after my death, no one can make you. Why do you want to save my life when it means giving up your chance at freedom?"

"I thought you were the one who was insistent about the fact that I'm your wife. I'm not a prisoner here."

"Answer the question. Why do you want to save my life when your success will mean that you stay married to me for the rest of our lives?"

She didn't know. She didn't have an answer that made any sense. All she knew was that the thought of any life after his death wasn't one she wanted.

"I'm your alchemist. You're my king. One of the most important things I do is keep you alive."

Taiyo narrowed his eyes and tugged on her hands, forcing her to step even closer. He shifted until he was on the very edge of the bed, her standing between his legs as he stared up at her. "Don't lie to me. You just said this has nothing to do with obligation. Why don't you want a chance to go back and marry someone else? Someone you love? The chance I took away from you. Why choose to save my life and choose me?"

What did he think he was getting at? Did he know nothing of her?

"Why would I want something I never had any intention of achieving? You didn't take a chance away from me when you married me. You can't take something away from me that was never going to happen. I was never going to fall in love with anyone. Any marriage I might have had would have been very much similar to ours, a practical, political arrangement with a clear purpose and no emotions or affection attached to it."

Speaking of, they were far too close for the bounds of a purely practical arrangement with no affection attached to it. She started to step back, but then his hands settled on her hips, curling into the silk and holding her directly in front of him. Her breath caught in her throat.

His eyes searched hers as he whispered, "Where have you hidden your heart?"

The heat of his hands even through the silk was distracting. Her mouth felt dry, which simply had to be because of how long they'd been talking. She swallowed, her own voice just as low. "The heart is just an organ."

"And yet... you still won't answer me. What are you afraid of?"

"Nothing." She narrowed her gaze at him, ignoring the way his fingers softly shifted. His thumb brushing back and forth had to be because he was trying to distract her, although why was beyond her. What bothered her more was the fact that it was working. She said, "All that matters to you is this: I am promising you now that in four months when the eclipse comes, you will survive it. I will save your kingdom. I will save your life. And I wouldn't tell you this if I wasn't certain. You can be certain of that. I don't give away hope lightly."

He stared at her for a moment, and she could still see him, searching and searching for the answer to why.

And then his hands on her hips were pulling her closer until she was in his lap and his head was pressed to her chest, the sheer capelet and nightgown the only thing between them, his arms wrapping around her. His ear was pressed over her heart and one of his palms rested in the same spot on her back. His other arm was locked around her waist so she was flush against him.

Heat flooded her cheeks, but Taiyo breathed out, causing the fabric to rustle. Her breath stuttered, and her admonishment never came out as he smiled. "There it is. Oh, and it is *racing*."

Hellebore could easily push him away. It would be no trouble. But she was certain her cheeks were a vivid red, and since there was still a little bit of the sunset left, she might as well wait until it was darker and his energy went with it. So she stayed where she was, reaching up and running her fingers through Taiyo's hair, twirling the orange and gold ends with her fingers and listening to his breathing.

She didn't care what it would take. In four months, she would not be seeing him into a grave. She'd sooner go in herself.

Why?

Hellebore never liked why. She avoided why. She preferred how. So why would have to wait.

CHAPTER 17

Haruko's presence in Hellebore's lab was not one she'd anticipated, but there her sister-in-law was, the door flung open, crashing into the wall while Hellebore leaned over Taiyo's shoulder, going over the healers' records of his condition that he'd brought with him.

Haruko's eyes darted around the room before they landed on them, the pair of them completely frozen.

Why was Haruko there and what exactly had she expected to come bursting in on? Hellebore elbow deep in his guts?

Taiyo, however, immediately rose from his seat and said, "Haruko, outside, now."

Then the siblings were gone, and Hellebore was thoroughly confused. There was no way Haruko knew that Hellebore knew about Taiyo's condition, given she'd only discovered it the night before. So what was Haruko doing rushing into her lab?

Elaine and Phoebe had been all a titter when Taiyo had joined her in heading to her lab. In the past he'd only

visited briefly to collect her to go to the garden. Although, it probably didn't matter how Haruko knew now that she was there.

Hellebore just picked up the records again and continued reading, ignoring the muffled voices out in the hallway. Soon enough, the door was flying open again and Taiyo was hissing, "—ko, don't!"

"Alchemist, if you think that you'll be running experiments on my brother without anyone to observe, you are sorely mistaken. While he might trust you with his life, I certainly do not!" Haruko came to a stop in front of the chair Hellebore was sitting in.

"You're free to observe, but don't even think of getting in my way." Hellebore lifted her gaze only slightly. "I won't let your desire to secure your son as heir to the throne stop me from saving my husband."

She received silence in response. Taiyo's expression shifted once more and he took a little, short breath, lips twitching up before he turned his head away.

Haruko narrowed her eyes, crossing the distance and glaring down at her. "My brother's life means more to me than it ever could to you. I won't let you steal his blood for your sick experiments while he trusts you wholeheartedly. I won't let you kill him."

"If I wanted him dead, all I'd have to do is wait." Hellebore huffed, pushing herself out of the chair. She fluttered the pages in Haruko's face, disorienting the elf and thus clearing the way for her to pass by and reach the table with her sterilized tools waiting for her to draw blood. "Not to mention, his blood is so thoroughly corrupted that there would be nothing I could do with it other than analyze it. I can't use his blood for my own benefit. You, on the other hand—"

"Haruko, Hellebore is the only chance I have. Trust me

on this, don't make this harder," Taiyo said, cutting Helle-bore off before she finished the threat as he took the seat beside the table.

Hellebore finished disinfecting her hands and moved to put on the sanitized leather gloves. She looked over her shoulder and said, "If it would help you feel more comfort-able about this and be closer to me, feel free to call me Hels. If I succeed, we'll be sisters by marriage for at least the rest of my life."

Taiyo rolled the sleeve of his shirt up to expose his left arm. He looked up at Hellebore. "Why haven't you told me about this little nickname?"

"You didn't ask, and then you made your own. Don't be greedy."

"Not one based off your name. I like Hels." Taiyo's eyes never left hers as she stepped closer, needle in hand, Haruko looking like she was going to be sick in the background.

"Of course you would, Hellebore is a mouthful." Helle-bore positioned the needle, finding his vein. "But if you get to use two nicknames, then you'll never call me by my full name again."

"I see." Taiyo smirked before it quickly turned into a wince as she pushed the needle in. He, however, never looked away from her face as she drew his blood. "This is just about how much you love the way I say your name."

Hellebore ignored his smug, teasing lilt and focused on her work. If Haruko got any greener, she was going to need a bucket. Taiyo's blood wasn't a pleasant sight, but was drawing a syringe of it really enough to make her so squea-mish and disgusted?

Hellebore finished, pulling the needle out and setting it to the side so she could clean and bandage his arm, fixing him with a stern look. "Your name is too short for a nickname, so it's hardly fair for you to get two and I none."

"You can always come up with one unrelated to my name."

"You really want me to start calling you sunshine?"

Haruko cleared her throat, nodding at the syringe. "What exactly will you be doing with that?"

"Analyzing it. I need to know the makeup of it inside and out if I'm going to find a way to cure it."

"What makes you think you can do this? You're not a healer," Haruko said.

"You should be grateful I'm not. Your healers for years have been trying and failing." Hellebore laughed and gestured to her lab. "I'm an alchemist. I'm the only one who can."

And that was that.

If Taiyo had been spending a fair amount of time with Hellebore before when she'd been focused solely on the plants, it was nothing compared to now.

He was always in her lab, at her side, either sitting in silence when she needed to focus or discussing his condition with her when she needed more answers or talking to her about any manner of things when she needed a break. He never complained when she needed blood. He never seemed worried each day that passed and she still didn't have an answer.

From sunup until sundown, they worked in her lab. Princess Haruko, after much convincing from Taiyo, had taken over his duties as king so he could focus on helping Hellebore save his life. They always left right before sunset. If a normal Sun Elf was weaker at night, Taiyo was doubly so. His heart had already been straining and struggling during the day to pump his thick, rotting blood through his veins, but at night it had to work twice as hard. Which is where the pain came in.

But the tincture the elven healers gave him didn't work well.

So within a week of examining his blood, Hellebore spent the night awake, a chair pulled up to his bed and an open notebook in her lap so that she could observe how his condition changed at night. All she could see was his expression screwing up in agony. His pained breaths and huffs were so soft, she understood why she'd never heard them before, but somehow the sound of them seemed to embed themselves into her mind.

She'd been working on the rot for months now and factoring in Taiyo's condition and his magic fighting the rot for a week. While her progress wasn't inconsequential on either end, it wasn't successful either.

She only had a little under four months left.

She made good on her promise to come up with a sedative to help Taiyo sleep without pain, this time ensuring the original tincture was fully out of his system before he took hers.

That first night she still watched over him, observing to make sure there were no side effects. The next night, as soon as he was out, she pulled her hand out of his and quietly crept out of his room and back to her lab. She continued working through the night.

She had to.

She couldn't add hours to the day, but she needed more time.

The next morning, she slipped back into her room right before dawn and put on the act of waking up for her maids when they arrived.

When Taiyo stood in the doorway connecting their rooms, waiting for Phoebe to finish braiding Hellebore's hair, he said, "Are you alright? Do you want to go back to bed? You look exhausted."

She forced down the yawn rising in her throat. "I'm fine. Just a little restless. Nothing a day in the lab can't cure."

That night, she hovered in the doorway, waiting for Taiyo to take the sedative so she could slip out again. But as he held the vial, he held out his other hand. "Why don't you stay, Hels? See if you sleep better here."

"I hardly think a few feet on either side of this wall will make a difference."

"No, but sleeping beside your husband might." He gave her a grin. "Who is asking so very nicely because he appreciates all the work she's doing for him."

Arguing with him was wasting precious time. If she refused, she'd have to come up with an explanation, and it would be so much easier if he would just take it and pass out.

"Well, when I hog the blankets, I expect no whining from you about it in the morning. You've brought this upon yourself," Hellebore said, stepping into the room and moving to climb into bed beside him. His mouth fell open at her acquiescence.

If he hadn't thought she'd do it, why give her the option?

He looked over his shoulder at her as he sat on the edge, ready to drink the vial. His eyes skimmed over her as she fussed with the covers, and there was something sad in them and something longing in his voice as he said, "Yes, I have."

Then he took the sedative and lay down, turning to face her as quickly as he could. He stared at her even as his eyes began to flutter. She was the last thing he saw before the sedative took him under.

His breathing evened out, and then Hellebore was carefully climbing out of bed and hurrying back to her room to change again and get back to her lab.

That night she watched her seventh attempt at the formula she needed to cleanse the irises of the rot fall onto the leaves, and nothing happened.

Hellebore's eyes watered beneath her goggles and she quickly stepped away from the table so she could remove them and scrub the emotion away. She took a few deep breaths. She might be cracking, but she would not break.

She could do this. She had to do this.

She pulled her goggles back on, opened her notebook, and recorded the results. She spent the rest of the night trying to break down what it had done and where to go from there.

She barely made it back in time to change and slide back into bed beside Taiyo before he woke up.

He stirred as she laid her head on the pillow, and she steadied her breathing, blinking her eyes right as Taiyo opened his, still facing her. He stared at her for a moment and his voice was thick and raspy from sleep. "You look exhausted. Did you sleep at all?"

"Good morning to you too. Hasn't anyone ever told you how rude it is to tell a woman she looks tired?"

"You're not just any woman. You're my wife. Your well-being is my concern."

Hellebore made a note that she was going to have to find some way to hide her exhaustion to throw off his suspicion.

"I'm also human. You're an elf. Sorry to break it to you, but this is what humans look like in the morning." She quickly flung the covers off and hit him in the face with them as she shot out of bed. "And I'm not even the one dying."

When he insisted on her sleeping in his room again that night, Hellebore went through the same routine, this time prepared, and the next morning he woke up and she received no comment from him thanks to the mineral she'd used her alchemy to turn into a cosmetic to hide the dark bags under her eyes.

But she knew this was unsustainable. She had to sleep at some point.

So that night, she came back early, her eyes drooping, and wrangled herself out of her clothes and into her night-gown and crawled back in next to Taiyo and let herself get a couple hours of sleep to tide her over for the next few days.

When she woke up, Taiyo was already awake, staring at her. "That's not the nightgown you were wearing last night."

Infuriating elf. Of course he would notice; he refused to take the sedative unless he was able to look at her while it took effect, and she was always the first thing he woke up to see.

"I got up in the middle of the night for some water and spilled it, so I had to change. Is that a satisfactory explanation or are you going to question why my hair isn't in the exact same place after sleeping on it all night too?"

She managed another two nights, slowly moving forward. She had just finished a blood thinner for Taiyo which would ease the strain on his heart and was a step in the right direction to a cure, but she could feel her exhaustion catching up to her. Her hands were shaking as she corked it.

They were shaking too much.

She tried to pull her hand back from the stand, but it was too late, she had no control. Her hand knocked into the stand and the vials went flying through the air. They shattered on the ground, the glass pieces spilling across the floor as the liquid ran across the stone. A whole night's worth of work wasted.

She sat on her stool and stared at the broken glass in silence for a moment. And at least there was no one around her to hear the embarrassing sob that fell from her lips.

No one was around to do anything when she cut her hands trying to clean up the glass so Taiyo wouldn't see it in the morning when she drew more blood. She bandaged her hands herself and went back to Taiyo's room early, climbing back in bed beside him. And if she was close enough to rest her good hand over his heart and hear its sluggish beat, no one was around to know.

When she woke up two hours later at dawn, Taiyo was holding her hand in his.

In hindsight, she should have been suspicious that Taiyo didn't ask her about her bandaged hand the next morning. She'd thought maybe he hadn't noticed it, given how his focus had instead been on the one resting over his heart.

Everything went as normal that day, and she was ready to take control of herself again and not waste any more precious time.

She was in her lab after having snuck out for approximately all of two minutes when the door opened, and she whipped around, beakers in her hands, to see Taiyo in the doorway, looking as ragged as he usually did at night.

Her breath hitched. She'd been caught.

Before she could even ask, he held up two vials, one full and one empty. He'd faked taking the sedative. "I don't even have the energy to be angry with you right now."

"Go back to bed, Taiyo." Hellebore moved back to her table, setting the beakers down and her hands on the table as she ducked her head so he couldn't see her expression.

"I'm fine. I'm making progress, and I need every second I can get if I'm going to save you."

"You need rest as well."

"You need a solution." Her voice cracked and she squeezed her eyes shut.

"I need my wife."

His arms slipped around her waist as his front pressed to her back while he curled around her. She could feel his breath brush her skin. "And I need her to be healthy and well rested, not running herself into the ground for my sake."

She tightened her grip on the table, not letting go. "I'll survive. You won't."

"I have the utmost faith in you. And even so, if I am in my last days, that means you should heed a dying man's request." He leaned down farther, resting his chin on her shoulder. He turned, pressing his lips to her neck, and whispered, "Come back to bed, sunshine."

She let go of the table, sinking into his arms. She whispered, "Only—Only because I'm getting sloppy without sleep."

Taiyo hummed as he lifted his head, brushing his lips against her jaw too slowly and deliberately to be an accident, causing her heart to stutter and him to smirk. "Of course. That's why your heart is racing right now."

"I'm sleep deprived and you startled me. It's—" Hellebore sighed as he pulled back, moving to take her hand in his and walk backward to the door. She said, "It's just a normal physical response to my state. It has nothing to do with you. I'm not coming back because you asked me. Don't think this means anything."

Taiyo's gaze never left her even as he reached for the door. "Believe me, I'm not that foolish. It'll mean something when your maids aren't the ones helping you out of your clothes."

Hellebore ignored the heat flooding her cheeks. "If you're waiting for any sort of affection from me, you will be waiting for the rest of your life. However long that might be. You're dying. You should be doing nothing that could hurt your already failing heart."

Taiyo laughed, full of the same bitterness as the blood that was coursing through his veins. "It is far too late for that."

She didn't like the way he was looking at her when he said that.

But they returned to his room and climbed into bed. Taiyo didn't take the sedative. Instead, the second she'd crawled under the covers an arm looped around her waist and she let out an undignified squeak as he pulled her to him. He breathed out a sigh as he settled against her back, curled around her once more. He muttered, "To ensure you don't get any ideas about sneaking off again."

Hellebore told herself when she woke up the next morning the only reason she was smiling was because of how rested she was from sleeping a full eight hours. It had nothing to do with the way Taiyo was tracing "sunshine" on her palm.

CHAPTER 18

At Taiyo's insistence, curing the irises was still Hellebore's highest priority, not saving his life. He was also watching her with an eagle eye and curling around her every night to keep her from sneaking away to keep working. Which only made the two months she had left all the more critical.

Hellebore had all the information she could gather about the rot, but none of the tinctures she'd created had done anything more than slightly slow the spread. Almost every plant she got her hands on had some version of the rot embedded into it, even ones that looked healthy.

She couldn't fathom how any person had been capable of this feat.

She'd had Taiyo explain it to her a thousand times and looked over his healers' notes twice as many times, trying to understand how he had taken on some of the rot in the first place.

What was the solution? If Taiyo's magic hadn't been enough to cleanse them, what would?

Hellebore looked up from the glass magnifying the

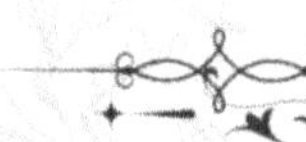

black roots and over at Taiyo who was lounging in his usual seat in her lab, alternating between his own work and watching her work. The second her eyes landed on him, he sat up, lowering the paper in front of him.

"Tell me the story of when you tried to cleanse the irises and ended up taking on the rot yourself."

Taiyo sighed, setting the report Haruko had given him that morning on the table. "Isn't it almost time for dinner?"

"Taiyo."

"I've told you more times than I can count."

"Tell me again."

Taiyo held his hand out, and Hellebore rolled her eyes but indulged him, leaving her samples so she could put her hand in his. The second her hand was in his, he pulled on it until she was in his lap, his other arm wrapping around her. He leaned back in the chair, one arm wrapped around her back and his other draped across her legs, giving her no chance of escape.

Hellebore hadn't had any idea just how touchy elves could be until the last two months. In normal circumstances, she wouldn't put up with it, but Taiyo was dying, and if it made him more cooperative, she'd allow some of it. The way she sank into him, leaning against his shoulder, was part of that. It had nothing to do with the warm rush that went through her every time Taiyo embraced her.

"How about a different iris story instead?"

Hellebore straightened up and started to squirm, ready to push herself away if he wasn't going to be helpful. "If you aren't going to help me save you—"

"I think you'll find this one worth your time, sunshine." Taiyo's grip on her tightened. "I promise I'll tell you mine again afterwards; just take a break and listen to this one first."

She settled back into his arms with a huff.

Taiyo laughed, thumb shifting across her skirts. "You've never asked me why the irises are such a sacred wedding tradition for us."

"I assumed it's because they share the same magic you do."

"Yes, but do you know why?"

Hellebore opened her mouth, took one look at Taiyo's mirthful expression, just waiting for her to spout off an alchemist's explanation, and snapped it shut. Then she said, "No. Enlighten me."

"A long time ago, back before alchemy had even appeared amongst the humans, and your people were busier killing each other than coming after any of us, we too were busy killing each other. The Sun Elves, the Star Elves, the Moon Elves, and the Night Elves. Everything changed when Agnarr of the Star Elves and his human witch discovered their comet and were able to create their ritual to bind all of the Star Elves' magic to it, doubling the strength of the weakest of the elf kingdoms. The Moon Elves formed an alliance with the Night Elves, and the king of the Sun Elves knew it was only a matter of time before we were at their mercy."

Hellebore sat up straighter. "Wait—Don't tell me, there was an eclipse coming—"

Taiyo squeezed her leg gently and cut her off. "Can you just let me tell the story?"

Heat flooded her cheeks. "Go ahead."

"The king had an unmarried daughter. He issued a challenge to his people. Whoever brought to him a way to strengthen their people in order to protect themselves from the Moon Elves and the Night Elves, he would give them the hand of his daughter in marriage. The princess was devastated to hear of this. She'd spent years dismissing every suitor that came her way, desperate to win her favor and hand in marriage, because she didn't love any of them. How could she? She was already in love." Taiyo paused, and even though Hellebore suspected where this was going, she didn't interrupt him.

"He was no one of consequence, really. Just one of the many gardeners who worked in the palace. As much as she loved him, she knew her father would never let her marry him, so she loved him in silence, determined that if she could not be with him, she would not be with anyone. Now that choice was being ripped away from her. Like most of the young male elves, he thought the princess was the most beautiful elf maiden he'd ever seen, but more than that, he had seen the way she laughed with her brother, how she always had a kind word for her maids, how diligent she was, every day coming to the gardens to practice and train with her magic.

"She was radiant to him, always full of light. Until the day after the announcement when he found her in the garden, sitting by the irises, sobbing over her fate. He listened, heart sinking further with every word. It was only a matter of time before one of the cruel elves she rejected presented something to win her father's favor and condemn her. She told him if only she could marry someone kind, like him, and before he could really even understand it, she kissed him. Then she hurried away, but hope lit in the gardener. His infatuation was not in vain, but what hope did a gardener have of presenting to the king something that could save their people?"

This was turning out to be a dreadfully romantic story. Taiyo couldn't have shortened it at least a little?

"Every day, suitor after suitor arrived at the palace, trying to impress the king with some new magic technique that was never really new at all. And every day the princess returned to the irises at sunrise and met the gardener. After wracking his brain, he finally came up with an idea. If the eclipse cut them off from their magic, then if they could find another source of sunlight to connect to, they would be able to use it to protect themselves. What better than an organism that already absorbs sunlight to survive? What if instead of wasting excess sunlight, it kept it? The gardener and the princess worked day and night trying to create a flower that would radiate sunlight with their magic, but no matter what they tried, nothing stuck.

"The princess began to lose hope, especially when the rumors began that an elf was coming with a weapon that would have the Moon Elves and Night Elves begging for mercy. The gardener, however, realized what was missing. The next morning, the princess came to the garden, ready to beg him to give up and run away with her instead because she could not bear the thought of living without him. Instead, she found the very first Sunrise Irises. When she realized how he had created them, her wail of grief tore through the castle. By the time her father and brother found her, it was too late. There was another swath of Sunrise Irises. As long as the irises survived, she and her love would be together. Her brother, in her honor, established the tradition, giving one to his wife on their wedding night to steward. As the irises began spreading throughout the land, so did the tradition. That's why they're so important to us."

Wait...

"That's it?" Hellebore startled. "They just both die?"

Taiyo nodded. "What did you expect?"

"I don't know. That he'd succeed and they live happily ever after?"

Taiyo's eyes softened. "It doesn't always work that way, sunshine."

"Well, that was a terrible story, so now you owe me yours."

"I didn't know you were such a romantic. I would have thought you of all people would have appreciated a tragedy." Taiyo's fingers brushed Hellebore's belt, fingers fiddling with the leather. "But if you insist—even though surely you've had it memorized by now—you know I was desperate to find a way to cleanse the garden and stop the rot. I believed that because the irises share the same kind of magic, only a smaller amount of it, that I could make a connection between myself and the irises with my magic and my magic would purify them. It helped, but the rot didn't disappear. All I did was transfer it into my magic and my blood."

Taiyo was right. She did have it memorized. But...

Hellebore immediately started scrambling out of Taiyo's hold.

"Hellebore? Hellebore!" Taiyo wheezed when her elbow connected with his abdomen as she forced him to relinquish his hold.

"I'm such an idiot!" Hellebore ignored him, successfully stumbling to her feet and racing for her worktable.

"What? Hellebore, what is going on?"

Hellebore grabbed her notebook, spinning around as Taiyo stumbled out of his chair after her, one arm wrapped around his stomach. She held it up as she grabbed a vial of decayed petals.

"I've been thinking about this all wrong. I don't have two problems to solve, just one!" Hellebore waved the petals in the air. "I don't have to cure you *and* find a way to cure the irises. I cure the irises and that is how I'm going to cure you!"

"Hellebore, I already told you that doesn't work. You don't have to—"

"Oh, will you stop it! How about instead you say, 'Thank you, my brilliant alchemist,' or 'How are you going to do that?'" Hellebore came to a stop in front of him again, beaming from ear to ear. "Why, my dear Sun Elf, of course I'll tell you. You got yourself into this mess because you thought of an idea only an alchemist could accomplish and went through with it with only your magic. Now you have rotting sludge for blood. I cure enough of the irises, then *I* use them before the eclipse to keep your heart from giving out. With enough irises, I can cleanse your blood. You couldn't separate the rot from the magic. Once I have healthy irises, I can."

Taiyo's hands caught her elbows, holding her in place in front of him, a grin on his face. "Your dear Sun Elf? I rather like the sound of that."

Had he heard nothing else of what she'd just said?

Also, where had that come from? The words had spilled out before she'd even realized it.

"Taiyo. Focus." Hellebore pulled out of his arms and shoved the vial into his face. "If I cure the irises before the eclipse, then I can use them to purify your blood before you lose your connection during the eclipse."

Taiyo blinked, reached up, and pushed her hand out of the way. A light started to flicker in his eyes. He breathed out, "My brilliant alchemist."

Hellebore laughed, dancing back out of his arms and back toward her worktable. "Fine. Don't thank me yet. Thank me when I have a cure for your irises."

Although her mirth was only surface level. The hope entering Taiyo's eyes cut her to the core.

He hadn't believed her until this moment that she could even save him.

CHAPTER 19

Hellebore couldn't have heard that right.

She looked up from the magnifying glass and whipped around to see Haruko in the doorway of her lab. Taiyo was holding the door, looking half-ready to shut it in her face.

"—stay long, you know I wouldn't ask you to stay long, but you've been shut away in here for months now, and they are whispering that you're afraid. Each whisper of the Moon Elves' movements or a sighting of a scout has them all in a tizzy. You need to be at this ball."

Right.

Hellebore had been so isolated from Chymes' court for the majority of each year over the last decade, she hadn't even thought twice about any functions she'd be expected to attend as queen. Or that Taiyo would still be required to attend them.

She hadn't so much as learned the name of a single noble in the months she'd been there.

Taiyo made a strangled noise in his throat. "Tell them I'm sick."

"And feed into the other rumors that you are deathly ill?"

"Well, are they really rumors if it's true?"

"Taiyo. Please, they will not stop hounding me about you and your alchemist and what you're doing hiding her away all hours of the day. Just for a few minutes. Act like everything is fine. Then you can go."

"I'll go, but I'm not subjecting Hellebore to their rumors and gossip."

"That's exactly what you'll be doing if she's not there."

Hellebore called out, "I'll go."

Taiyo whipped around and Haruko raised an eyebrow, like she hadn't even noticed Hellebore in the shadows, trying to determine if the tincture she'd given the potted iris was actually curing the rot or if she was seeing what she so desperately wanted to.

Taiyo stared at her in stunned silence. Haruko recovered first, clearing her throat and nodding. "Excellent. Then I'll see both of you tonight. I'll have your maids prepare you accordingly, alchemist. I'd suggest getting started on that soon."

"Haruko—" Taiyo started, but she was already gone.

"Don't worry, Taiyo, it's just for a night." Hellebore pulled the glass away from the plant. "Besides, you're the one who is always getting onto me about not working too much."

"Technically, it is work, for both of us. And it's the last thing I would have expected you to volunteer for."

Hellebore took her gloves off and started for the door, grinning as she ducked under his arm and into the hallway. She tucked her gloves into one of her pouches. "I live to surprise."

Taiyo followed her out into the hallway, but she was

already turning down the hallway, throwing behind her, "See you tonight!"

The second Hellebore arrived back at her room, Phoebe and Elaine were already there, practically bursting with excitement at the chance to do more than just braid her hair or help her into a complicated nightgown.

As Hellebore closed her eyes, letting Phoebe pour water over her head as she washed her hair, she could hear the unspoken question in the air.

Why?

An excellent one. Up until this point, Hellebore had shown no interest in any of the Sun Elves or being part of the court. Why now?

While Phoebe and Elaine were exemplary servants enough to never voice their question, Hellebore knew it was only a matter of hours until she would have to answer it when it came from her husband's lips.

Her husband...

She blinked past the water still running down her face and looked over at the iris. It sat in its place, soaking up the sunlight. Hellebore had been caring for it as was expected of her, even when no one was watching and when she'd never be allowed to use it.

The only iris she'd ever seen that hadn't caught the rot.

Even if she failed to cure the rot, would that one iris be enough for her to save Taiyo?

If she did kill the sacred plant to save his life, would he forgive her?

Why did it matter so much to her? When had he started mattering so much to her?

Hellebore focused on the one question she knew she would be asked and could at least answer later.

Phoebe and Elaine fussed over her for hours until everything about her was perfect. As perfect as she could be for a human amongst elves.

Hellebore brushed her hands over the top tier of the full, silk skirt. The peachy-orange sleeves were practically molded to her arms, complementing the gold detailing on the bodice.

She looked over at the Sunrise Iris sitting off by the window.

They were an almost identical match.

"You look beautiful, if I may be so bold, Your Majesty," Phoebe said, clasping her hands together and beaming.

Hellebore supposed she did. She looked like a Sun Elf, just missing the pointed ears. She looked like she actually belonged there.

Did she?

Before she could examine it or herself further, Phoebe and Elaine were rushing her off to meet Taiyo for their grand entrance.

Taiyo was pacing in front of the doors, ignoring the footmen pointedly watching him as he moved. Hellebore's breath caught in her throat at the sight of him. He always dressed regally, but ever since stepping back from his duties somewhat to be at Hellebore's disposal, he'd been dressing a little less formally day to day. Now... he was dressed as only a king should be. His circlet rested on his head, a pristine white suit jacket fitted perfectly to his chest, and on top of it, a Sun Elf style Hellebore had no name for, only that it matched her dress in color and style.

They were a matching set.

They looked like they belonged to each other.

Taiyo paused and looked up at her approach.

His eyes widened and she heard his breath catch audibly as he froze in place, eyes desperately running over her figure.

She resisted the urge to wrap her arms around herself to hide from his intense gaze. Instead, she came up to him, held her arms out and said, "So? Do I make a decent elf?"

Taiyo blinked several times before her words got through to his brain. He stepped back, ducking his head before looking back at her. "You don't look like an elf."

Hellebore's lips started to turn and she looked down at her dress, but before she could reevaluate, a finger came under her jaw and lightly tilted it back up. Taiyo was barely a breath away. He whispered, "You look like a queen, sunshine. My queen."

"T—Taiyo—" Hellebore didn't know why she was so out of breath even though she'd done nothing at all. She didn't know why her voice caught and stuttered over his name or why her cheeks were flushing a brilliant crimson even under the makeup her maids had put on her face.

His thumb brushed her lip for the briefest of seconds before he pulled it back, taking a deep breath and glancing over at the footmen, their eager audience. "We're ready; open the doors."

Taiyo looped his arm through hers and Hellebore pushed every confusing, ridiculous feeling away. If she was going to be facing the court for the first time since her wedding, the last thing she needed was any emotions distracting her and putting her in a girlish tizzy.

The next hour was a whirlwind. Everything seemed to blur the second after the herald called out her and Taiyo's names as they descended the stairs into the ballroom.

She spotted Haruko and her husband across the room, Haruko raising her glass and giving Hellebore a cold but approving nod. Good to know it was possible to get her sister-in-law's approval.

Then it was noble after noble in front of them, music filling the air, as everyone was eager for a chance to get their claws into their king who'd been mysteriously absent as of late. A few of them were more eager to get their claws into their human queen.

Taiyo never once let go of Hellebore's arm.

She didn't know if that was for her sake or his.

What she did know was that she didn't mind being attached to his side.

Hellebore did notice the instant Taiyo's condition caught up to him. His tone became more clipped. His grip on Hellebore tightened.

So Hellebore leaned in, cutting the lord off and demanding some water for her parched throat. The lord's response was only stunned silence until Taiyo cleared his throat. "Your queen has made a request of you. It would be wise to fulfill it."

The lord scurried off and Hellebore spotted three more vultures moving to take his place. She lowered her voice. "Come on, you need to go. The sun will be setting any moment now, and you need rest."

Taiyo took in a slow, deep breath, but she could see the frustration in his eyes. "There's a door to our left. We'll have to go the long way then."

If that's what it took to escape the ballroom and get him back to his room so he could rest. Hellebore took the lead, noting the directions more nobles were coming from and skillfully weaving her and Taiyo through the crowd, dodging any attempts to catch their attention until they were finally through the door and free.

Hellebore immediately grabbed Taiyo by the shoulders and started looking him over. He waved her off. "I'm fine. Just tired, that's all. I'm not about to keel over right now."

"You'd better not," Hellebore said with a huff. She looked around and then put her hands on her hips. "Well, which way?"

He laughed, grabbing her arm and running his fingers down it until he laced them with hers and started walking. "This way. We'll have to go to the ground floor and go around."

"Like around outside?"

Taiyo looked over his shoulder and grinned. "Is that a problem?"

"I think some fresh air would do you some good."

"Probably, but I've just spent all night trying to think of ways to get you outside so I can see you and that dress in the sunset."

Hellebore pulled her hand out of his, rolling her eyes as they started descending the stairs. "At some point, you'll get tired of all that."

Taiyo looked back at her even as he continued taking the stairs one by one. "Of you? Never."

What was the point in arguing with him? She wasn't even sure what she was really arguing for, only what she was arguing against.

She took a deep breath when they stepped outside the castle, basking in the lingering warmth and glow of the sun as it began to descend. True to his word, Taiyo stopped and stared at her, painted in the pink and orange glow of the sky.

The longer he did, the less the warmth she felt came from the sun and more from the rush that went through her when she had his undivided attention like this.

Finally, he shook his head and started walking, throwing over his shoulder, "Definitely worth it."

She hurried after him as they wound their way around the castle, passing by and through the public gardens until she spotted a familiar hedge. She grabbed Taiyo's sleeve and tugged on it. She pointed to it and said, "That's the iris garden, right?"

Taiyo nodded, coming up to it. He reached in and nudged a few branches to the side, revealing a path into it. "This is a more secret entrance. I've let it mostly grow over in the last few years, but I keep just enough of a way through that it still exists. It's not good for a place to only have one exit. Should an enemy corner someone here, it's an escape. Hellebore, wait—"

But she was already slipping through, doing her best not to snag her skirts or bodice on the branches. She stepped into the garden and the stench of the rot overwhelmed her all over again without her mask to filter it out.

She turned as Taiyo followed her. She gestured to it and said, "Why didn't you tell me about it?"

"I didn't think it was relevant."

If both entrances were guarded, but only one was locked with a key...

"Do you think that's how the Moon Elves got in here and introduced the rot?"

Taiyo gritted his teeth, crossing his arms. "I don't know."

Hellebore turned on her heels, looking at the last remaining patch of irises, all on their last legs. They were closer to the main entrance. Taiyo had said the disease had started closer to the main entrance and that patch was one they'd tried to protect.

Why protect that patch, closer to the contagious flowers, rather than the ones farthest away from the disease?

Why—

She whipped around and looked up at the castle. She could hear the music from the ballroom in the distance and it was *not* helping her think.

She took a deep breath, looking back at the irises. If only one of them was healthy enough for her to be able to use just as a baseline to know if her cure was working on any level. It wasn't the soil itself, but the roots—

Hellebore let out a yelp as she was swept up in Taiyo's arms, spun around in the garden as he said, "Dance with me, sunshine."

"What?" Hellebore clutched his arms until he set her back on her feet, hands on her waist and his face blocking her view of the irises.

"You promised me you didn't need to work tonight, and we went to our first ball together and didn't even have the chance to dance. Please, dance with me before the sun finishes setting and I won't have the energy anymore."

"Taiyo, if that's your reasoning, you shouldn't be dancing at all. You're just trying to distract me because I started thinking about the irises. We'll just go back—" Hellebore started to pull out of his grip, but he only wrapped an arm around her back and pulled her closer.

"Just one, Hellebore, please," Taiyo whispered, and she froze. "I'm not so fragile I can't dance with my wife once."

His hand settled on her waist as his other found hers and took the position for a Chymesian dance Hellebore was thankfully passable in. He took the first step and she responded, taking the proper position as she whispered, "Why?"

Taiyo hummed along to the music, eyes locked onto hers as he moved them through the steps perfectly. "Does a husband need a reason to want to dance with his wife?"

She breathed out, unable to look away from him even if she wanted to. "You know that's not what I'm asking."

"I don't think you know what you're asking, sunshine."

He lifted his arm for her to twirl under, her skirts fanning out, sending pieces of decay fluttering through the air. The sun continued its vibrant descent, and Hellebore could not pull her gaze away from her husband's face, practically glowing in the light even as his exhaustion crept in.

He was beautiful, obviously. He was an elf. She'd have to be blind not to notice, and yet, somehow she didn't think she truly had until now.

What was she asking? And did she really want to know the answer?

If she did, she'd have to respond.

And she still didn't have a cure for the irises, which meant he was still dying.

"Answer me, now, why did you volunteer so quickly to come to this tonight?" Taiyo murmured, tugging her closer until she was flush against his chest. Her heart hammered against her ribs, and why couldn't the dreadful organ just beat normally?

Her mouth went dry, but at least she had prepared for this. "I have every intention of doing exactly what I swore I would do. Once I cure the irises and use them to cure you, well, I'll still have, hopefully, another sixty or so years. If I succeed, we both have a life after this, and I won't be able to avoid actually being your queen forever. I'm just getting a head start."

Taiyo's movements slowed, not ending the dance entirely, but no longer matching the pace of the music in the distance. "So you have been thinking about a future with me."

"I'm not so short-sighted as to not have even spared a few minutes to realize what happens if I succeed."

"But even before you knew my life was at stake, you had no interest in building any kind of future of acting as queen, only as my alchemist. What changed?"

Well, she hadn't prepared an answer to that question. She was silent a few moments, finally able to avert her gaze, ducking it so she stared at his shoulder.

No clever answer came to her lips. No cold justification was hiding deep within her mind.

"I... I don't know."

"It's not a failure to not know," Taiyo whispered.

Hellebore's throat tightened and water started welling up in her eyes. She was supposed to know. She was an alchemist; the whole point of her existence was to find answers. The only reason she was there in his arms was so she could give him answers and save his kingdom.

She blinked the tears away and looked back up at him. "You didn't answer me."

"I will when you're ready to hear it." Taiyo came to a stop, keeping her pressed against him. He lowered his forehead to hers, his breath brushing her cheek. Her heart raced wildly even as his beat a slow, sluggish tempo. His eyes fluttered shut and he breathed in deeply in the final pink rays as the sun disappeared behind the horizon. "Tonight... just let me hold you."

She could close the distance between them. It would be so easy. His lips were only a breath away from hers. He wanted her to. She could feel it in the slight shake of his arm curled around her back. He desperately wanted her to.

But he wouldn't do it.

She closed her eyes.

She wanted to.

But she couldn't do it.

Hellebore took a soft, shaky breath and pulled her head back. Her eyes opened and she reached up, brushing her fingers over Taiyo's cheek. She whispered, "The sun has set. You've overexerted yourself."

Taiyo nodded without opening his eyes. His hands didn't leave her.

She had to reach behind herself and gently pull them

away so they could leave. She had his hands in hers when he finally opened his eyes.

"I love..." Taiyo's voice was a broken breath, as faint as the music in the distance. "I love when you wear our clothes and our colors."

Hellebore dropped his hands. "They're... They're just not practical. I'm an alchemist."

"For now?"

The hope swelling in those two words had Hellebore's stomach turning.

"I don't know."

Why didn't she know? What was she doing? What was she feeling?

Hellebore and Taiyo made it back to their rooms in the dark. She should have never offered to come to this ball. She should have stayed silent and in the shadows of her lab.

She discarded the ballgown on the floor and started to pull on a nightgown, moving to do the buttons when her eyes flickered over to her iris, glowing dimly and illuminating the room.

She still had several buttons left when she saw it.

A small brown and yellow spot on one of the leaves of her iris.

Her knees hit the ground with a jarring thud as she dropped to them in front of the iris. Her mouth fell open, and a strange half-gasp, half-sob tore out of it before she could contain herself.

The door between their rooms slammed open. "Hellebore?"

But she couldn't pull her gaze away from the Sunrise Iris, not even as her husband ran into the room. Her fingertips brushed the leaf as her vision blurred with the water spilling over them. "T—Taiyo—"

"What is it? Hellebore, what—" Taiyo rushed through

the room, until she saw him freeze in the corner of her eye, catching himself on the bedpost. All he had still on were his trousers, his other finery discarded like hers.

She pulled her shaking hand away lest she do any more damage. A sob started rising again despite her best efforts to push it down. Her hand curled into her chest as she lost the fight against her tears.

His arms were around her once more. He pulled her into his chest, turning her head away from the iris.

"I'm sorry—Taiyo, I didn't—Please, believe me, I didn't—"

He clutched her to himself, hand rubbing up and down her spine as he gently shushed her, murmuring, "It's not your fault, sunshine. I know. You did nothing wrong. It's alright. I promise. Everything is going to be alright, you'll see."

Hellebore couldn't find any more words; all that came out were wretched, keening sobs as Taiyo started rocking her. She buried her head against his chest, his skin warm against hers. She pressed her ear against his heart, sobbing with every painful, slow beat of his heart as it fought to push his blood through his body.

Was each beat just the seconds counting down until his time ran out?

Was trying to save him as hopeless an endeavor as trying to keep the iris from catching the rot?

Where had this agony come from? Why was the thought of losing him tearing her apart from the inside out?

How was she going to live if she failed to save him?

CHAPTER 20

Hellebore woke up the next morning like every other morning as of late, curled up in Taiyo's arms, listening to his heartbeat. However, this time, when Taiyo ran his fingers through her hair and whispered her name, she did not respond.

She could not save him with useless tears. She could not turn his blood red again by almost kissing him. These feelings were distracting her, and he was the one who would pay the price.

If the pain she felt at failing the iris was any indication of what she would feel if he died...

Hellebore needed to put a stop to this now.

So it was for his sake she untangled herself from him with only a cold, "I need to get to the lab."

"Hellebore—"

But she was already in her room, locking the door behind her.

Thankfully she did because she heard the knob rattle as she shed the nightgown she'd never even finished buttoning.

"You *locked*—Hellebore, can we just take a minute and talk? It's not your fault! It was a miracle there was even an iris out there that hadn't caught the rot in the first place. It was only a matter of time before the rot reached it. You couldn't have prevented it."

She steeled her heart and focused on tucking her blouse into her waistband.

"I know I made a big deal about taking care of the iris in the beginning, and—I wish—sun above, Hellebore, I wish I could explain. This was out of your control. You haven't failed me or our marriage or anyone because it's sick. Hellebore? Sunshine?"

She buckled her belt, hands trembling.

"Are you in there? Will you please say something?"

Hellebore finished buckling her belt and whirled around, throwing open the door. He was still dressed only in his trousers from the night before. She looked him over with a cold, calculating edge. The same way she examined a vial. "You should get dressed. Or take the sedative and go back to bed if you're in pain. Either way, I don't need you this morning. I'll be in the lab."

Then she shut the door in his face, grabbed the newly rotting iris, left through her main door, and told herself the panging sensation in her chest was simply imagined because all that was there was an organ pumping blood.

Hellebore spent the morning in blissful silence, mixing a new variation of her last tincture that had brought healing but had not been strong enough to rid the plant of the rot entirely. She also snipped off a still healthy bloom and a few leaves to examine. That afternoon as she was distributing it to her potted test irises, her wedding iris right beside them to also receive a dosage, the door to her lab opened. She lifted her dropper and tilted it up to avoid any unintended droplets from falling as she looked at the door beneath her goggles.

Taiyo stood in the frame, mouth open but eyes locked on their iris waiting for a dose.

His voice came out frigid as he said, "What are you doing?"

"There's nothing special about it now. Now it's just another iris to cure. So I might as well start using it. It's early on in its rot, the earliest I've had my hands on. It could be the key to cracking this whole thing."

Taiyo took a small step into the room. "What is wrong with you?"

"I don't know what you mean," Hellebore said, turning back to her first iris and finishing the dosage.

"Last night you were sobbing in my arms about it, and now it's just another test subject to you? You've spent months taking care of it and the first hint of rot had you unravelling but now you supposedly don't care?"

Hellebore set the dropper aside and recorded in her open notebook the dosage she'd given her first subject. "I wouldn't go that far. If I didn't care, would I be trying to save it before the rot continues to eat away at it?"

Taiyo didn't respond, jaw clenching as he stared at her.

She ignored him and moved to administer the dosage when a hand wrapped around her wrist and pulled it back. She gasped as Taiyo pushed between her and the iris, twisting her wrist just enough to force her to let go. The dropper hit the ground, liquid spilling slightly as she stared up at him.

Hellebore took a deep breath, pushing down the burning sensation rising as the precious tincture lay on the ground. "What is wrong with you?"

"Me? The first chance you get, you're the one ready to

tear our iris to pieces. I spent last night trying to comfort you and convince you it wasn't your fault, but you were just upset you didn't have a perfect specimen, weren't you? Have you been sneaking pieces of it away and studying all along? Is anything sacred to you? Does anything actually matter to you?" Taiyo hissed, letting go of her wrist. "Or is it just the second something finally does mean anything to your frigid, steel heart, you get scared and you'd rather destroy it than let it have any chance of hurting you?"

His words cut right through her.

She couldn't let them.

"You came to my country, demanding my hand in the hopes I'd be able to cure your irises. You got me. You don't get to complain now about getting exactly what you asked for. What do you want more, for me to let that iris rot and not touch it simply because you tell me it's supposed to matter to me? Or would you rather I use it while I can to save the rest of your irises, your people, and your life?"

Taiyo pointed to the blunt marks where she'd cut off a bloom, voice burning. "You swore. You swore to me on our wedding night you would not hurt it. You would not turn it into an experiment."

"I kept my word, even though this isn't a real marriage." Hellebore reached for her goggles, pulling them down so he could see her whole face. "Until now."

"Until it wasn't convenient."

"Convenient certainly isn't going to all this trouble to save the life of the Sun Elf who kidnapped me and forced me to marry him and is now yelling at me because I'm prioritizing practical measures to do so over some silly little tradition that came about because two elves were foolish enough to believe they were in love."

Taiyo made a noise in the back of his throat, then

grabbed the edge of the table behind him. "Why didn't you just tell me? Why didn't you ask me this morning about using our iris?"

"The thought didn't occur to me. Besides, your answer wouldn't have mattered."

He gestured at her. "That. That right there is exactly what I'm talking about. You and your walls and your impossible pride! At every turn, you refuse to let me in! Just when I thought—" Taiyo cut himself off, hand falling to his side. "I thought..."

"I will own my mistakes when I've made them. I should have been clearer as of late. I should have made this evident the moment I discovered your condition and that you are intrinsically tied to all of this. Here is the truth. We alchemists will study living creatures and organisms. My specialty, as you know, was plants, but I have also done more than my fair share of study on creatures in a lab. You think I knew how to separate the sedative from your body while it was already in your stomach by luck? It took me three dead rats before I managed to successfully master the technique. You think I could have learned as much as I have about rot if I cared about the plants I introduced it to? Back at the academy, I never once saved a sick plant. I killed them. I have been valiantly attempting the opposite in this case, but the principles that guide me now are the same as back then."

Hellebore came to a stop right in front of him. He gripped the table tightly, leaning back from her.

"The most important principle for alchemists working with living creatures? Never, ever get attached to them. An attached alchemist is no alchemist at all. They won't have the stomach to do the terrible things they need to in order to advance."

She hadn't seen that horror in his eyes in so long. The

turning of her stomach and sweeping chill over her wasn't real. The sensations would pass.

"That's what I am to you? An experiment you can't afford to get attached to?"

Hellebore nodded.

"And what about thinking of a future with me? What's all this been about then, if you insist there is no possibility you could care for me?"

"Purely practical thinking. As for the rest... I'm putting in the work to try to keep you from dying. That should be enough."

"It's not." Taiyo let go of the table, reaching for her arm. His fingers gently curled around her bicep as his voice lowered. "I want more."

"I am afraid I don't know what you mean."

He grabbed her other arm and pulled her closer, bringing his forehead down to hers. "Don't pretend to be stupid. You know exactly what I'm talking about. I want a real marriage. I'm *tired*. There's still the strong possibility I'm going to die. From before I laid eyes on you, I knew I would marry you and die. If I don't have long left, I don't want to spend it in a sham of a marriage."

Her breath hitched despite her iron will.

"Why, you can ask. Why have I been doing this, all of this all this time? Knowing who you are, who you are so similar to in so many horrible ways, I still could not help myself. I could not stop myself from wanting this to be something real. I don't want to *die*—"

Taiyo's voice cracked and his grip on her tightened. He was trembling against her.

All this time, even as she'd been insisting upon saving him, he had an air of peace about him. Any time he talked about his possible death, never so much as a crack.

She wasn't the only one who'd been trying to be emotionless.

She reached up, placing her hand on his side. He took a deep, shuddering breath. The orange ends of his hair brushed the collar of her blouse.

"I don't want to die," he whispered again, eyes squeezed tightly shut, as if it was the first time he was truly letting himself say it and mean it. "But... I especially don't want to die before ever having a real marriage."

If he'd said this any other time, or if he were human, she would have understood his meaning far differently. But this wasn't about consummation.

"Taiyo..." Hellebore whispered. "I can't... I... What I can give you is your life. That's the hope. I succeed, and I save you, and all of these fears of yours are for nothing. Because I'm going to die, and at worst, you're only going to have to wait about sixty years, and to you that'll be so little time. You'll have half of your life for you to have a real marriage. You don't need to force yourself to make do with me. You'll marry a beautiful Sun Elf, and you can tell her she has me to thank for the fact that you're even alive to be the wonderful husband you will be to her."

Taiyo opened his eyes, taking her face in his hands, eyes burning once more. "Is that supposed to be a comfort? Do you think I've been holding you in my arms every night and I'm not tormented? Can you not see how desperately I want you to save me so I can be with you a little longer? And, yet, at the same time I'm torn because if you do, it means one day I will lose you and have to spend decades mourning you. I do not want some marriage with someone else. I want *this* marriage. I know the difference between wanting to be a husband and wanting to be your husband."

"You just..." Hellebore breathed out. "You just believe

that because you've convinced yourself of it. You're a good, loyal elf. You think these things because you feel like you have to. Eventually, you won't be able to convince yourself any longer. You can dress me in your people's clothes all you want, but that doesn't make me a Sun Elf."

"I don't want you to be." Taiyo's fingers slipped from her cheek to her ear. She shivered as he gently ran his fingertips over the rounded curve. "You are the one who needs to be convinced. For someone so smart, you are so willfully blind. Do you not see how beautiful you are to me? Do you not realize the power you have over me? Have you not seen how any time you come before me in my people's clothes and colors, you bring me to my knees? Not because you look like an elf, but because you look like you are mine."

"Is that all you want? Possession? Is that what will satisfy you?" Hellebore couldn't stop her voice from turning into a weak, breathy sound.

"You've made yourself clear today. So have I. You know what I want. I know what you think you can't give. But you don't have to be Palladia. You don't have to shut me out. You don't have to fear any attachment to me. I'm not your experiment. I'm not one of your plants for you to desiccate. I am your husband."

Taiyo pulled his hand away, letting his fingers drag across her skin until they finally parted. His hand hovered in the air for a moment as he walked backwards, away from her and the rotting irises. He curled his fingers in and then let his hand fall, eyes burning into her.

"And since you refuse to accept it, and you're afraid of caring for me because you fear you'll lose me, take the iris. Use it. Save them. Save me. Once you no longer have to fear losing me, I will be here so you can finally show me where you've hidden your heart."

Hellebore was alone again, useless organ pounding.

She took a deep breath. Focus. Once she'd saved him, she could prove to him he was wasting his time trying to wish her into a wife that could love him.

182

CHAPTER 21

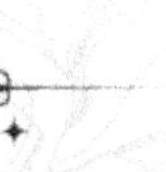

Hellebore only had a month left. She pushed aside all emotion and immersed herself wholly in the rot.

Any time Taiyo tried to raise a concern, she gave him a cold look and told him that if he didn't want to die, he needed to trust her. With how little time there was left, it always shut him up.

She was getting closer; she could feel it in her bones.

She could see it in the rotting irises. She had the right components. She just didn't have the right ratios.

She needed to figure out what combination would be powerful enough to cleanse the rot away without killing the irises as well in the process, while also needing a tincture that would revive them within a small number of doses. She'd tried experimenting with a longer time period, but even at a lower dose, too many doses just killed the irises without killing the rot first.

She was nose deep in one of her old notebooks, reading by candlelight in Taiyo's bed. He had one arm draped over her side, fingers idly playing with the silk fabric of her nightgown. She ignored his gaze on her. She'd told him to take the sedative and go to bed, but he stayed awake, just staring at her.

She flipped the page, and he groaned softly behind her.

"Keep that up and I'll pour the sedative down your throat myself."

"You wouldn't."

"You're right, I wouldn't." Hellebore looked over her shoulder at him, lifting her arm to show him the charcoal in her hand. "I would transmute it into you before you could stop me."

He pressed his hand flat against her stomach and in a swift move, shifted them both until he was leaning against the headboard and she was against his chest, sitting between his legs. He rested his head on her shoulder, murmuring into her ear, "If you insist on reading this when we should be sleeping, then you'll have to endure me reading it as well."

"Be my guest," Hellebore said, sighing. "Maybe you'll see something I've missed."

She continued reading her account of her research from her last year at the academy. She had never been able to put her finger on why the rot affecting the irises was familiar to her. It didn't act the same way the types of diseases she'd studied did. Was it because the plants were magical?

No. If that were the case, it wouldn't have been affecting the other plants the same way. It was something about the rot itself.

She flipped a page and Taiyo stiffened against her when some of the first words were "Aunt Palladia."

She looked at him out of the corner of her eye as he skimmed over the page detailing how Aunt Palladia had been helping her develop a way to transmute the disease into a portable form to be able to potentially turn it into a weapon by poisoning an enemy's crops.

His arms around her waist tightened just a hair, but it was enough of an excuse for her to lower her notebook and shift so she could see his face fully.

"Alright, seriously, when are you going to tell me what happened between you and my aunt?"

He sighed, leaning his head back against the wood. "I've been trying to wait for the right time. It's… I don't want to fight."

"Is there something to fight about?" Hellebore asked, setting her notebook to the side.

"She's your aunt."

"Yes, I am aware of that. I've spent a good portion of my life trying to be her."

Taiyo's eyes narrowed. "You and your aunt could not be further apart. You are not like her."

Hellebore raised an eyebrow. "Now, we both know that's not true."

Taiyo fell silent.

She whispered, "You just don't want me to be like her."

Again, she was met with silence.

"Do you think I'll automatically take her side?"

"It's… complicated. I want to tell you…" Taiyo sighed. "When I first met her… it wasn't long after I had just become king. Haruko and I traveled to Chymes when your father took the throne. It was my first time ever having to be king outside of Iubar."

"And my aunt can smell weakness a mile away."

"I was idealistic. I was young. So young, I was almost still a child in my people's eyes. If your people had understood how we mature in comparison to yours, they would have seen me as one. I wanted to believe the best of Chymes, that the alchemists weren't still the same as they had once been in the stories we'd been raised on. Haruko thought I was foolish and insisted on coming with me. Your father wasn't friendly, even then, but he was what I'd hoped for. A king of the alchemists who wanted to have a good relationship with Iubar and keep war from happening between us again. I... I thought your aunt was of the same mind as your father. I trusted her. I shouldn't have."

"You were an unfortunate casualty then of her disagreements with my father. I don't think either of them have ever agreed on anything."

Taiyo snorted softly. "It was more than that. I should have known better. I should have listened to Haruko when she tried to advise me, but I wanted to believe differently."

"What happened?"

"Your aunt... she never saw us elves as people. She looked at us the way you look at your plants."

The tension in his voice silenced any follow-up questions she might have had. Whatever her aunt had done to him or Haruko, maybe it wasn't something to speak about.

Everything was starting to make more sense.

She lowered her voice. "I shouldn't have said you were an experiment."

"You didn't mean it," Taiyo whispered. "I know you didn't."

"Still, for what it's worth, I'm sorry."

Taiyo shifted again, pulling his gaze away. "Don't... Don't."

What?

Hellebore watched as he stared at his desk in the corner. "I'm not... I'm not innocent. I... I've used what happened in the past to justify myself time and time again. But that doesn't change what I've done or make it right."

"Taiyo, what are you talking about?"

He turned back to her. "If I was in the wrong, what would you do?"

Had both he and her aunt been guilty twenty-five years ago?

"You mean like the things you did in order to marry me and secure my help?"

"Yes. Hellebore, if I told you... If I had done something awful, truly despicable... If I hurt you, would you forgive me?" Taiyo closed his eyes. "Or would you let me die?"

"I'm not letting you die."

"But would you forgive me?"

"Do you want to put your life at risk by telling me something you know will make me angry with you and distract me from focusing on this cure? Or will you let me focus on curing the irises and trust me to figure the rest out afterwards?"

Taiyo nodded.

"Besides, I refused to let you die even when I thought you were actively kidnapping me—and you were—and I got over it eventually. Have a little faith."

She squirmed out of his grip just enough to set her notebook to the side and blow out the candle. As they both settled back down to sleep, Hellebore rested her head on his heart to measure the beats. He ran his fingers through her hair, brushing his thumb over her rounded ears. She was thankful the darkness hid her blush.

"Speaking of afterwards," Taiyo murmured, "maybe you'll be ready to write to your brother? Or even invite him here? Surely you can't stay mad at him forever."

"One problem at a time. Go to sleep."

Hellebore was fairly certain she was the one who fell asleep first as Taiyo's ministrations steadied her.

Whatever it was... if he was able to forgive her for using

their iris, surely his secrets couldn't be so bad? And if they were... Well, Hellebore would have to save him first to find out.

CHAPTER 22

In all Hellebore's life, she had never worked harder at anything than she did during the last month she had to save the irises and save her husband. She was both hardly conscious of anything, the days all blurring together, and also conscious of everything as her mind spun in a million different directions; the well-developed habit of meticulous notetaking and recordkeeping of experiments drilled into her from a young age was the only thing saving her.

Each day that went by without a cured iris, Taiyo's protests about her overworking herself and her health got weaker until they vanished completely. She felt it in the way he held her at night. She knew it from the tears that occasionally fell onto her skin in the darkness. It was burned into her from the way his hands trembled against her.

He didn't want to die.

Hellebore brushed her fingertips over the sloped, pointed edge of his ears. She ran her fingers through the orange ends of his hair. But she never had the words. She was trying.

It wasn't enough.

She couldn't give him what he wanted. She couldn't even give him what he needed.

He probably wouldn't even get the honor of being turned into a fond folktale. No. He'd be a cautionary one. So the next generation and the one after that and all throughout time knew better than to rely on an alchemist, and certainly to never marry one.

Just another Sun Elf tragedy.

The king with a rotting heart and his alchemist wife without one.

Just over a week before the eclipse, and after several weeks trying as many different ratios as she could, Hellebore and Taiyo walked into her lab and she let out a choked gasp.

Taiyo quickly wrapped his arm around her waist as his head whipped around, but she grabbed at his arm, shoving it away and racing toward the table. "Look! The iris!"

Taiyo raised an eyebrow but followed her. "What about it?"

She picked up the pot and practically shoved it at him. She gestured to the leaves. "Look! Its color is back! This was the third dose, and the rot is gone and the iris is alive!"

He looked up, a smile twitching on his lips. "You did it."

She set the pot on the table and turned back to him. She whispered, a smile tearing across her face, "I can cure the irises before the eclipse. I can save you before the eclipse."

Taiyo stared at her for a moment. She opened her mouth to repeat herself to ensure he understood what that meant, but then his lips were on hers and she was stumbling back into the table to catch herself from the force. One hand of his caught her, palm splaying out against her back as his other tangled in her hair, cupping her cheek and steadying her.

Before she could even rationalize her own actions, her hands found his waist as she kissed him back, heart racing and elation flooding her.

It was a wild rush.

The success of her alchemy. Finally having something to prove she wasn't worthless. Taiyo's devotion. It was overwhelming, it was too much all at once and not enough.

She'd never felt anything like this before.

Would she ever feel anything like it again?

Why was she kissing him back? Why did she never want to stop? Why did she so desperately want this—want him for the rest of her days?

She was breathless when he finally pulled back, thumb brushing over her cheekbone as that intense longing was fixed wholly upon her, and she had nowhere to run from it now.

He breathed out, "Do not speak. Do not breathe a word to me, sunshine. Let me have this."

She did not. She stayed silent.

"Let me have—" He leaned in again, pressing a kiss to the corner of her mouth before dropping to her jaw. "—this one moment—" Then her neck. "—where I can pretend my desperate, aching love for you is met with the hope you can return even just a fraction of it."

He pulled back up to look down at her once more. "You know… Hellebore, you must know I love you with every beat of this rotting heart. And you must say nothing. You will not say anything to me, do you understand? You will not pretend a heart is just something that pumps blood when you hold mine in your hands. You will just… Just let me love you."

"Taiyo—"

He kissed her again, and whatever she'd been about to say was gone. All she could feel was him and his heart beating beneath her fingers and the certainty that within a week it would be twice as strong.

But her heart was beating against her ribs, and if she wasn't an alchemist, she would swear that she could hear it screaming at her, begging her to let it out. To let her husband take it and keep it all the days of her life.

He pulled back once again, this time eyes closed and forehead resting against hers as he whispered, "Please, wherever you have hidden yours, at least let me give you all of mine."

And she did as he asked. She said nothing. She just closed her eyes and tried to steady her own heart back to where it should be. Could she? When this was over, could she finally be able to tell him something more than "I don't know"?

Could they be something more than a tragedy?

None of it would matter if she didn't finish the job and save him anyway.

His love would be a waste if she could not ensure he had more than a few days left to make use of it.

* * *

Hellebore was up to her elbows producing enough of the tincture for it to be delivered across the kingdom in time for the irises to be back to full health just in time for the eclipse. Haruko oversaw the distribution and riders and wagons were in and out of the courtyard every five seconds the same way Hellebore's maids and the other servants were in and out of her lab every five minutes to collect the next batch. Taiyo made a surprisingly competent assistant, ensuring she was able to keep up with creating the supply needed for a whole kingdom.

By the time they'd finished, with only one batch left,

she shut the door behind Elaine and looked over at Taiyo. He hovered by the last batch. He raised an eyebrow. "Is this just in case?"

"I thought... I thought we might do the garden here together." Her voice came out weak and breathy and an unsure smile flickered across her lips.

He lit up brighter than the sun, and within seconds they were out the door with the last batch. They would have run through the halls—totally unbecoming of two monarchs— if there wasn't the risk of dropping the batch of vials. Instead, they went as fast as they dared until they came through the door and stepped into the rotting garden. With their droppers and their vials they went iris by iris until they had distributed it all. Taiyo turned on his heels. "How long until it'll take effect?"

"By tomorrow morning we should see them start coming back. And within three days..." As Hellebore looked around, she took a deep breath. All these irises, would they be enough to cleanse Taiyo's blood? They had to be. There was no other option. "We'll be ready to start on you."

But even with her confidence, it was only a theory. What if she was wrong? Now that the chance to try was within her grasp, what if she still failed?

That night, Hellebore's head rested on Taiyo's chest, listening to his heart sluggishly thudding along.

What if she still lost him?

She could not sleep. She could not wait for dawn to begin ironing out the details. She hoped Taiyo would forgive her this one last time sneaking away with the eclipse bearing down on them.

She ducked into her lab, checking in on the only iris left. The only one in the castle brought back to full health, still missing the bloom she cut off it. Her wedding iris. The others had been taken and sent to the farthest edges of the kingdom, closest to the Moon Elves so they could use them in an attack.

She brushed her fingers gently over the petals. If it was supposed to be some superstitious symbol of the health of her marriage, what did it say that she'd healed it?

Hellebore opened up her notebook and carefully measured how much magic her Sunrise Iris held. If every individual iris had a level around that average... Or was it based on the number of blooms? If the more blooms there were, the more magic they held, the better. If each bloom held around the same amount as hers...

Were there enough irises in the garden to cleanse him?

She was not going to be able to sleep peacefully by her husband's side until she knew exactly how many blooms the garden had. She'd sleep when Taiyo wasn't dead.

She ran through the empty halls, notebook in one hand and key in the other to the secret passageway. But when she reached the corridor, instead of the smell of rot greeting her, it was something else.

Something worse.

Smoke.

She ran faster, flinging open the door, yelping as the metal knob burned her. She was immediately blasted with a painful, searing heat. Hellebore recoiled instantly, eyes watering and stinging from the smoke. She coughed and opened her eyes to see the massive flames tearing through the garden.

The orange and red flames were blinding, making it impossible to see anything else.

No.

It was because there was nothing else to see. Everything that mattered had already been overtaken by them. The whole world in front of her was on fire.

Hellebore's whole world was up in flames.

All the irises were burning.

Taiyo's life was burning before her eyes.

Hellebore screamed, clutching the castle as the boiling heat and the flames creeping toward her hem kept her from being able to run into the garden. Her knees buckled as tears spilled over and her keening tore through the night.

The fire raging in front of her didn't care.

It just kept burning.

Taking her husband with it.

She clutched at her heart. She'd been right. Oh, how much she wished she hadn't been. Seeing the rot on the iris was nothing compared to this agony.

How—How could this have happened?

No one else knew where this was save for Taiyo, Haruko, and Hellebore.

Water. She had to at least put it out before it spread to the castle. Maybe there were some there she could save. Maybe some alchemy she could do to—She fumbled for her charcoal and started to flip to an empty page.

No. First, she needed to alert someone and get back before she could try transmuting any water in the atmosphere. She spun around, ready to keep screaming the castle down for help when she crashed right into two familiar figures. The Moon Elves.

Before she could do anything, one grabbed her head and the other stuck a needle into her arm and was injecting her with the same sedative she'd once given to Taiyo. Her legs crumpled beneath her and the first elf caught her as her eyes fluttered shut.

"Sorry, Hels, no time to explain."

But why would a Moon Elf speak Chymesian?

CHAPTER 23

Something wasn't quite right, but Hellebore was groggy, and she really didn't want to confront whatever the strange feeling was that was under her skin. She would rather stay in Taiyo's arms for a few more moments.

Except when she rolled over to shift closer and listen to his heartbeat, there was nothing there. She stretched her hand out only to come up against rough wood. That was what wasn't right.

There was no one lying beside her. No arm around her waist. No fingers tracing words across her skin. Taiyo wasn't there.

She ripped her eyes open and scrambled to sit up with a sharp gasp and Taiyo's name on her lips. But when she opened her eyes, his name died in her throat. She was in the back of a wagon. That was when it all came rushing back. The fire. The Moon Elves.

The irises were gone.

Worse, so was she.

"Perfect timing, Hels, we're almost to our camp for the night."

Hellebore blinked and looked at the two Moon Elves driving the carriage. Except, they weren't Moon Elves anymore. They were wearing the same clothes, but the silver of their hair was fading back to their natural colors, brown and blond respectively.

It was night, but the moon hanging overhead provided just enough light to see.

"Callahan? Emerson?"

Callahan eyed Emerson and said, "You didn't get the mixture wrong and scramble her mind, right?"

"Of course not!"

Hellebore got her legs under her and crawled up to the front of the wagon where the two of them shifted so they could see her better. She gestured to their clothes and said, "What do the two of you think you're doing running around pretending to be Moon Elves?"

"Hellebore, keep up; so no one traces your disappearance back to Chymes," Emerson said with a snort.

Her mind was spinning. "Wait, so the two of you grabbed me in the garden." Her stomach sank and the flashes of fire haunted her. Her voice lowered. "Did you two set the fire?"

Callahan and Emerson exchanged a look, and she smacked their arms. "Out with it! You drugged and kidnapped me, burned months of my work to the ground—you owe me an explanation!"

Taiyo.

Without the irises, she had no way to stop his death during the eclipse. How long had she been under? How long did she have to find a miracle to save him?

"Well..." Emerson said, reaching up and scratching the

back of his head, causing even more of the silver coloring they'd used to rub off.

Callahan sighed. "Yes, we set the fire. You weren't supposed to be there at dawn. The fire was supposed to be a distraction so then we could find you, grab you, and escape while the Sun Elves dealt with that."

"Whose brilliant plan was that? You didn't have a key to the garden, so how did you find the other entrance?" Hellebore's voice rose as Callahan pulled the wagon to a stop. "Do you know what you've done?"

"Obviously, Hels, it was all me, and you know I never do anything without knowing exactly what I'm doing."

Hellebore gasped as Aunt Palladia's voice filled the air. She looked to see they were at a small camp, and her aunt was standing by the fire, arms outstretched.

Callahan and Emerson climbed down while Hellebore hurried to the back, shooting out of it before either her brother or her former beau could help her. She went running toward her aunt, but instead of running into her arms, Hellebore smacked them out of the way. "No! You *don't* know what your plan has just done! As much as I want to be elated to see all of you—some of you for the first time in half a year—I can't! You need to take me back."

Palladia grabbed her by the arms. "Hels, you need to breathe. Sit down, and let me explain everything. Can you do that?"

Not when every second brought her husband closer to death and her family had just destroyed her hope of a solution.

"I don't have time for this! I'm already at least a day away from the capital. By the time I get back I'll only have four days at most to find another way to save him. I have to go now, just give me a horse." Hellebore ripped herself out of Palladia's grip and started back toward the wagon, ready to loose one of them, but Callahan and Emerson stepped in her way.

Callahan held his hand out. "After the trouble we went to getting you out, we can't let you go running back in. Not to mention you're not making any sense. Save who?"

Oh, if she had the time, she'd be tearing Cal to pieces for everything he'd done. Or asking him why on earth he was there kidnapping her when he had agreed to her marriage in the first place.

"I thought you were smarter than this, Hels," Palladia said with a sigh, shaking her head.

"Smarter than what?" Hellebore turned back to look at her aunt.

"You fell for his lies, didn't you?" She clicked her tongue, voice softening. "It's not your fault, Hels. He's very good at them."

Emerson leaned in and whispered to Callahan, "Do you know what they're talking about?"

Hellebore didn't know what Palladia was talking about.

Palladia sighed, putting her hand on Hellebore's shoulder. "Oh. He never told you, did he?"

Hellebore looked up at the moon, Taiyo's voice whispering in her ears.

"*I'm not innocent.*"

Then...

"Told me what?"

Palladia gestured for her to come to the fire. "Come here, and I'll tell you everything. He's been keeping us from rescuing you since the day he kidnapped you and forced you to be his bride with his lies."

Hellebore looked at Callahan, narrowing her eyes. "You agreed to the betrothal. That's what he told me."

Callahan stepped forward, glancing between Palladia and Hellebore before wrapping his arm around her shoulders. "Do you think I would ever truly let an elf run off with you as his bride without even speaking to you? You were supposed to be my alchemist, not some elf king's consort."

Callahan *hadn't* agreed? He'd wanted her to be his alchemist?

In a daze, she let her brother lead her over to their aunt, who pulled her to sit beside her and by the fire. Callahan and Emerson took seats around her, so she was fully encircled by them. She whispered, "I don't understand. Father sent a letter through Taiyo—"

"Hels, we've been trying to rescue you from him since the beginning," Callahan said. "Emerson and I rode as fast as we could, trying to beat King Taiyo to the academy so we could find you first and get you out of there before he found you."

Oh. She'd assumed they'd been riding ahead with a warning for her to prepare herself, but this whole time they'd been riding so hard to help her escape.

"But... the negotiations. Why didn't you protest then?"

Callahan squeezed her shoulder. "I wanted to. I tried to reason with Father in private, knowing I'd only make things worse if I tried to defy him publicly, but he would not listen to me. You weren't there. The Sun Elf king... he was ruthless. He swore that if we didn't give him your hand in marriage, there would be war, and he would not be anywhere near as merciful as his predecessors had been. That first day, he looked right at our father and told Father that he owed him your hand. I couldn't make any sense of it, but it was all set into motion before I could stop it."

Was that what Taiyo had meant? He'd been bluffing, obviously—given their bigger concern was the Moon Elves, he wouldn't start a war with the alchemists.

Callahan shifted so he was facing her, and she steeled her heart even though it had only been a few months ago she'd been sobbing, desperate to see her brother again. Now all she could think about was Taiyo.

"I didn't stop there. We received word he'd found you and was taking you to Auror for the wedding, and I set off before the messenger could take even a step to carry the news to Father. I rode as fast as I could and I made it to Auror the night before, but I was foolish. I thought my standing as crown prince would at least get me inside the gates and a chance to see you where we'd find some way to escape. I was taken by the guards the second I gave my name and brought to a holding cell. At dawn, the Sun Elf king finally deigned to see me, but he refused to let me see you. He wouldn't even let me attend the wedding. He kept me there until the next morning when his guards threw me out of the city."

Taiyo hadn't... No. It couldn't be true, but...

Haruko, the morning of the wedding... *"My brother has been unexpectedly occupied this morning..."*

It fit. Taiyo... Taiyo had known her brother had come for her. And he'd never said a word.

"Let me guess, Hels, you never once received a letter from me, did you?"

Hellebore's voice cracked. "You wrote?"

Callahan's expression darkened. "I knew it. If he wouldn't even let me see you from a distance, of course he wouldn't give you any of my letters, no matter how innocent I made them sound on the surface."

He'd *known.* This whole time, Taiyo had known her brother hadn't abandoned her and he'd lied to her face. He'd taken the letters. He'd let her believe that her brother thought she was worthless.

Hellebore squeezed her eyes shut, throat tightening painfully. She'd cried more the last six months than she had the last ten years.

"Hels?" Callahan whispered.

"Is she crying?" Emerson whispered with a panic she'd never heard in his voice before.

She covered her mouth with her hand. She was among her people again. Crying was a waste of time and energy, but she couldn't make herself stop. Her voice broke into a sob. "Cal—I'm so sorry—I thought—"

Then her brother pulled her into his arms and she clutched at his shirt, crying into his shoulder. Her brother held her tightly, nearly crushing her in his grip as Hellebore's world went up in flames a second time not even a full day later.

How could Taiyo have done this? How could he claim to love her when he lied to her? *Why* had he lied to her? Why would he have hidden her brother's letters one hour and then the next been encouraging her to write to him?

Would he have even sent it if she had? Was it just to try and raise her estimation of his character in her eyes so she would want to save his life?

Did she know Taiyo at all? Or just what he wanted her to know?

Hellebore was still shaking, trying to stop her sobs, when Callahan pulled back, bracing his hands on her shoulders and locking eyes with her. "You have nothing to be sorry about. That elf is the monster here. He lied to you. He took advantage of you. That's not your fault."

Hellebore nodded, taking one last breath before managing to finally win against her tears. Callahan squeezed her shoulders. "Chin up. You're safe with us now."

Aunt Palladia cleared her throat, and Hellebore instantly reached up, wiping away her tears. She straightened back up, pulling out of Callahan's grip. Emerson had averted his gaze, and Hellebore almost laughed at the absurdity of it all. Six months ago, she wouldn't have known what to do either. Or worse, she would have been rolling her eyes at the excessive display of useless emotion.

"Your brother is right." Palladia waved her hand as she came closer. "Do not waste a moment blaming yourself for that creature's deception. I knew the second that creature arrived at my academy what was happening. He was finally coming to finish what he'd started twenty-five years ago. The best way to make me suffer would be to take you from me and make me helpless as he used you."

If Taiyo had been hiding her brother's letters, what else hadn't he told her? Had he been afraid she'd take her aunt's side because he'd been the one to wrong her all along?

Hellebore was starting to believe anything was possible now. She didn't know him. She never had, had she?

CHAPTER 24

Palladia reached forward and took Hellebore's hands. "I'm so sorry you were caught up in all of this. I'm so sorry it took us so long to rescue you. I can only imagine what he's done to you these last six months."

Wait...

"Done to me? Aunt, he's done nothing to me, I assure you—"

"Hels, he has lied to you, used you, and manipulated you all so you cannot see him for the monster he is." Palladia shook her head, not letting go of her hands.

Hellebore fell silent. Maybe she was right.

Hellebore needed to know the truth. She couldn't pretend it didn't matter anymore.

"You are not the first princess and alchemist he tried to capture and bind in matrimony."

Now that—Of all the things she could have imagined, that was not it.

"Shortly after the old king of the Sun Elves died, so did my father, making your father king. That was when our

kingdoms convened to reevaluate the terms of our truce as was standard. King Taiyo and his sister arrived, no desire for true peace in their hearts. All they wanted was to get revenge for a centuries-old grudge by taking a princess and alchemist and subjugating her to the humiliation of being married to an elf. I was just about to take my position as the King's Alchemist but hadn't officially received the position when the idea was put forward. A marriage alliance. Your father's reasoning was that it would make us truly allies and finally put to rest all the bad blood between us. He really just wanted to get rid of me. But I wasn't about to let either of them get away with it. I wouldn't let the elf king trap me and force me to be his bride."

Emerson eyed Palladia for a moment before whispering to Callahan, "Wait, seriously? She was engaged to the elf Hels is married to? Um, ew."

Hellebore was more focused on her aunt's story than Emerson's commentary. "What did you do to break the engagement without sending us to war?"

"I made it clear to him that I was not some little human he could toy with. He did not respond well. Thankfully, I was much cleverer than him, and the leverage I secured was what I bargained with in order to break the engagement. I escaped Auror and while your father was displeased, I refused to let him sell me off to that monster. By that point, there was nothing your father could do about it. The elf king had no interest in a wife that wouldn't let him run roughshod over her. I did what I had to in order to protect myself, but I thought that was the end of it. I never imagined he'd try again with you. Or that he would succeed."

Hellebore took a deep breath. She couldn't cry again in front of her aunt. Once was already unacceptable. Twice?

"You... You make him sound like some kind of evil, scheming mastermind," Hellebore whispered.

"I trusted her. I shouldn't have."

"She looked at us the way you look at your plants."

"You have proof before you twice over that he is. Hels, he is very good at putting on an act. I'm grateful I never once fell for it, but I don't hold it against you for letting him get to you."

Who did she believe? Taiyo, who'd been lying to her for months and preventing her brother from reaching her, or her aunt, who had been diligently trying to rescue her since the second Taiyo had slung her over his shoulder?

It should be an easy choice. There was clearly a right answer.

But...

"Aunt, twenty-five years ago, he was basically sixteen and you were thirty."

Callahan's side of the story had been completely honest. She had no doubt about its veracity. Her aunt, however... wasn't telling her everything.

Callahan's eyes widened and Emerson muttered, "Oh, that's worse."

Palladia raised an eyebrow. "That doesn't change his nature."

Her aunt couldn't even at least be a little remorseful at taking advantage of his trust?

Hellebore had been so blind.

"Oh, yes, I'm sure he was thrilled to be engaged to a woman who was twice his age in development and maturity and that he had orchestrated all of it to get revenge for something that happened centuries ago rather than facilitate peace!" Hellebore ripped herself out of Callahan's grip. "Oh yes, I'm quite certain he was manipulating you when he showed you the secret entrance to a sacred garden of Sunrise Irises, trusting you with that only for you to curse it and his kingdom with a rot that has lasted twenty-five years!"

Hellebore should have seen it sooner. She should have figured out ages ago who had been behind it. It'd been painfully obvious, if only she had been willing to even consider it. She'd assumed it was the Moon Elves, and he'd never corrected her.

If he had, would she have taken Palladia's side?

"You're just repeating the lies he told you to win your sympathy. I know you're confused—"

"He didn't tell me anything about this. He never told me what you did, probably because he feared I wouldn't believe him. But it's the only thing that makes sense. You were the one manipulating him." Hellebore pushed herself to her feet, and the three around her quickly rose as well, blocking her in. She glared at her aunt. "You're trying to make me believe he's the villain when it's been you all along."

Callahan grabbed her shoulder. "Hels, you didn't see him when he came to the capital, trying to do again exactly what Aunt Palladia describes he did twenty-five years ago. Did you already forget what I just told you? If he was innocent, why wouldn't he tell you the truth? Why would he run out after discovering you weren't at the academy and kidnap you and force you to marry him? Why would he refuse to let me even enter the city the day of the wedding? Why would he stop all of my letters from reaching you?"

"But how can I be certain I can believe *you*?"

Callahan shifted back, heartbreak filling his eyes. "Why would I lie? Do you really think I would ever abandon my little sister to a monster? Do you really think I would have chosen Emerson to be my alchemist over you?"

Everything Callahan was saying was what she wanted

to believe, and why would he lie? Why would Taiyo do that to her?

He claimed to love her...

Had he just been manipulating her? Trying to get her to fall in love with him by pretending to be in love with her?

She looked over at her aunt. "Did you poison the irises or not?"

Palladia lifted her chin. "I did what I had to in order to protect myself. The elf is the one who brought it on himself."

"If I hurt you, would you forgive me? Or would you let me die?"

Hellebore looked up at the moon, traveling through the sky.

She didn't know. She didn't know who to believe. But she did know one thing—if Taiyo was dead by the end of the week, she'd never have the chance to find out.

"Take me back," Hellebore whispered.

No one responded; they just stared at her.

"Take me back to my husband."

Callahan let go, stepping back while Emerson shifted his weight from foot to foot. Palladia crossed her arms.

"Fine. I guess we're doing this the hard way. Emerson."

Emerson grabbed Hellebore and she gasped. "No! Emerson—No! Please—"

But his grip was too strong, and before she could stop him, another syringe was in her neck. The sedative.

She tried to push him off her, but it was already taking effect. There was no fighting it.

The next time Hellebore woke up it was morning, and her hands were tied behind her back as she was lying in the wagon as they loaded it up.

Callahan sat next to her in the back while Emerson drove the wagon and Palladia rode ahead.

Hellebore blinked her eyes open at her brother, who was staring at his hands. The same expression on his face as when he'd been caught by their tutors cheating on his assignments. Guilt.

He noticed her shifting, glanced over, and his expression soured further at the sight. She muttered, "Let me guess, Emerson ran out of the paralytic he transmuted into my blood four months ago?"

"Sorry about that," Callahan whispered.

"Why didn't you tell me it was you coming for me?" Hellebore tried to sit up. "I thought it was a trap."

"It needed to look like one so the Sun Elves blamed the Moon Elves; that way we could hide you away," Callahan muttered. "The masks were designed so if anyone came across us, they wouldn't be able to tell we were speaking Chymesian. We just needed to grab you and get you out and then we were going to explain. Clearly necessary since you've been brainwashed and won't come willingly."

"You believe our aunt over me?" Hellebore whispered. "I am telling you, Taiyo trusted her and she betrayed him. She's started the rot that's been hurting his kingdom for twenty-five years, and it's killing him. She's lucky her actions didn't start a war. That's why he did all of this. He needed an alchemist to clean up Palladia's mess."

"I don't care what happened twenty-five years ago, Hels. I care about you. I care about the things he's done to you, isolating you, manipulating you, using you as some sick, twisted revenge on our aunt. I've been beside myself with worry about what he's been doing to you these past six months."

"Cal, he needs me. I won't defend him keeping you away and hiding your letters, but I won't condemn him to death for it. If you don't take me back, I'll never get answers. He'll never have the chance to explain himself. Right now, he needs me. You've got to let me go."

"Why do you care if he needs you? Why do you want to go back and hear anything that monster has to say?"

Hellebore didn't like why.

The sun was rising in the sky as they set off. Before Hellebore could come up with an answer that made any sense to her or her brother, something shifted in the trees. Palladia whipped around, reaching into her belt, but before she could, a horse came tearing through the brush. Hellebore gasped.

"Taiyo."

CHAPTER 25

Hellebore couldn't look away as Taiyo and his steed came to a screeching halt before barreling into them. He'd come after her.

Why?

Because he needed her? Or because he loved her?

Did he even know the difference?

Even if he got her back, didn't he know the chances she could save him were next to none?

His eyes landed on her and he took a short, quick breath, something flickering in them before he turned to Callahan and narrowed his eyes. "You will return my wife to me this instant, and I will forgive you the lapse in judgment and forget about this as a favor to her."

Callahan crouched in front of her, one hand out as though Taiyo was something she needed to be protected from. "And all the lies you told her? Keeping me from seeing her and destroying my letters? Was that a favor to her too?"

Taiyo's jaw clenched and his horse pawed at the ground. He wasn't denying it. He looked away from

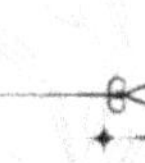

Callahan and locked eyes with her. "Hellebore, do you want to go with them?"

She started to move forward, opening her mouth, but Callahan grabbed her and pulled her back. "Taiyo—"

"If I wasn't going to let you take me, what makes you think I'd ever let a creature like you have my niece?" Palladia brought her steed between Taiyo and the wagon, hand in one of her belt pouches.

The softness that had entered his expression vanished as he laid eyes on Palladia. "You have tested the limits of my patience and my mercy for the last time, Palladia. Give her back."

It was sunrise, so Taiyo's strength would be returning, but he'd nearly died trying to rescue her from Callahan and Emerson four months before. He was weaker than he'd been then and he would have to fight Palladia too.

"See, I don't think so. Looking at you now... I think I just have to wait a few more days and then you'll be dead, and my niece will be free."

"This isn't about Hellebore or any goodness in your heart. If you really just wanted that, you wouldn't have taken her from me days before the eclipse. You're trying to take everything from me again."

Hellebore stared at Palladia's back. Had her aunt always been this way?

Had Hellebore been that way?

She needed to get out of this.

"That would require her being yours in the first place."

Hellebore could see the words pierce him right in his rotting heart.

She opened her mouth again, but Callahan clapped his hand over her mouth. He hissed in her ear, "Stop it. Let me and Aunt Palladia handle this. You're too emotional and easily manipulated by him."

Taiyo's voice darkened. "Enough. If you will not release her to me willingly, I will be happy to take her back by force."

Palladia grinned. "How romantic, but I have a better idea. I have something you want even more."

Hellebore stilled, slumping against Callahan, whose brow furrowed.

"The only thing you have that I want is my wife."

"Really? See, you don't look well, elf. And given how determined you are to get an alchemist back under your control... I think I know exactly what you did." Palladia pulled out a glass vial and held it up to the light.

Taiyo blanched, eyes widening, and Hellebore startled even as Callahan kept her in his grip. Within the vial was a dark red liquid, and Hellebore knew the formula etched into the glass well.

Blood.

Taiyo's blood.

Palladia tilted it back and forth, watching the liquid shift. "Which means I know how invaluable this is to you. Let's make a deal. You leave and never set eyes on my niece again, declare her dead or something in an attack on the eclipse, and I give you this little vial and your healers can use it to save you. You'll have no need for an alchemist anymore, and I'll graciously call us even."

Taiyo's expression twisted into a deep scowl. "You heinous—"

"Ah! Is that any way to speak to the alchemist holding your only hope of survival in her hands?"

"You think I'm foolish enough to trust you now? After you have revealed yourself to be a duplicitous snake three times over?" Taiyo's grip on his reins tightened, and she could see them shaking.

"Don't blame me just because you didn't measure how much you gave me in the first place."

Hellebore's mind was spinning. What were they talking about? Had Taiyo given Palladia his blood when they'd been engaged?

Was this the leverage she'd mentioned?

Is that what he'd meant by trusting her? Why would he have done that?

"You expect me to believe you now when every word out of your mouth is a lie? How do I even know that's my blood and not a fake? Or that it's not poisoned like before?"

Palladia grinned. "I guess you don't. But with only a few days left before you croak, do you really have a choice? It's your only hope now."

What was she doing? Even if Taiyo took the deal and got his blood back, his healers wouldn't be able to use it to save him. Only an alchemist would be able to, and even then, with how little there was and how far gone Taiyo was, that was a slim hope at best.

But Callahan's palm over her mouth kept her from being able to shout to Taiyo not to take it.

"I would rather spend a few hours with my wife than take that blood and spend a lifetime without her. I won't repeat myself again. Let her go."

Palladia's fingers curled around the vial and she sighed. "Such a shame... Well, sort of. I do so love getting my hands dirty."

In a blur of movement, she tucked the vial back into her pouch and reached into another as Taiyo lifted his hand up and began summoning sunlight.

No matter what, Hellebore couldn't let her aunt kill her husband. She would not let them take her from him.

Hellebore bit Callahan's hand right as Palladia threw the pellets, transmuting them into smoke. The last thing

Hellebore could see clearly was Taiyo's horse rearing up and Palladia charging forward, pulling her mask up.

Hellebore started coughing immediately as Callahan held her tighter. "Emerson, now!"

The wagon started rolling, and Hellebore jolted, ripping herself out of his grip. A light ripped through the smoke, and in the near distance she could see Taiyo's silhouette in the haze.

"Hels, no—come back!"

She felt Callahan scramble to grab hold of her, but she threw herself out the back of the wagon and tumbled to the ground. A jarring pain rattled up her shoulder as she landed on it, but she quickly rolled off it and stumbled to her feet. Her hands were bound behind her and all she had on was a nightgown, no belt or weapons.

She coughed, tucking her head into her shoulder. All she had to do was reach Taiyo. Then they could escape together.

She could hear Callahan and Emerson behind her, so she took off toward the sunlight cutting through the smoke. Her eyes burned and she called out between coughs, "Taiyo!"

A scream ripped through the air, but it was too high-pitched to be Taiyo's. The smoke was starting to clear and Hellebore could see her aunt holding her right arm in front of her, burned so badly the glove was melted into her skin. If she could see Palladia, Callahan could see her.

Hellebore ran faster as Taiyo fell to his knees, wheezing as he pulled two dissection knives out of his side. Four knives littered the ground where Emerson had missed him. Black blood bubbled up and poured out, staining his clothes and skin as he dropped the knives. Hellebore crashed to her knees beside him, shoving her wrists into his face. "Quick, get this off, I'm of no use to you without my hands!"

Taiyo fumbled with the rope for a moment, still wheezing until he grabbed one of the knives and cut through the cord. Excellent.

The second her hands were free, she grabbed the rope and the knives, pulling them together in front of her. The ground, however, wasn't soft enough for her to legibly write in. There was too much grass.

Her aunt ripped the leather glove off with a vicious shriek as Callahan and Emerson reached her. Hellebore didn't have much time left.

Squeamish alchemists didn't last long.

Hellebore ignored Taiyo's pained exclamation as she hurriedly shoved her fingers in his bleeding side. With her other hand she grabbed his metal buttons and ripped them off, throwing them beside the knives. She wrote the formula on the silk nightgown and pushed her power into it. The formula glowed, and the transmutation succeeded. She grabbed her weapon, scooping up the rope and stumbling to her feet in front of Taiyo, spinning it just in time.

Callahan yelped and jumped back right before the spiked ball attached to the end of her rope nearly slammed into his chest.

Hellebore kept spinning it, forcing all three of them to keep their distance or else risk finding out just how much it would hurt to feel it slam into them and rip their skin to shreds as she pulled it back.

She felt Taiyo's hand curl around her leg and he breathed out, "Hellebore—"

Callahan held his hands up in the air, not getting any closer, but not retreating. "Hels, please, we are trying to save you!"

Palladia took something out of her pouch and threw it

to Emerson. With her right arm burned beyond repair, she wouldn't be able to transmute easily. "Get that into her system and be done with it."

The sedative.

Hellebore gave herself more lead on the rope and aimed. Right at the same time as Hellebore's spike ball hit his hand, a small burst of blinding light appeared in front of Emerson's face, causing him to cry out and recoil. The bundle of herbs fell into the dirt and Hellebore looped the ball back around. It crashed into Emerson's chest, tearing through his skin and sending him farther away from the sedative.

Palladia hissed and started hurrying for it, fumbling for a piece of chalk with her left hand. Even with only one hand, Palladia was not going to let them go.

"Taiyo, get on the horse!"

"Hellebore—"

But she was already moving into action, her spiked ball almost crashing into Callahan, who avoided it only because he threw himself out of the way, skidding across the dirt. She dropped the rope and dove for the sedative, curling her fingers, still black and slick with Taiyo's blood, around it.

Palladia dropped the chalk, clawing at Hellebore's arm. "What a disappointment you've turned out to be."

Hellebore grabbed the chalk with her free hand, pressing her clenched fist into her chest as she looked over her shoulder. "I was going to say the same."

She elbowed her aunt in the nose and then slammed her foot into her charred arm, causing her to scream. It gave Hellebore just enough time to write on her own arm the formula. The sedative disintegrated beneath her palm as it transferred into Palladia's blood.

Hellebore stumbled to her feet as Palladia slumped to the ground, the sedative flooding her veins. Emerson was blinking furiously, injured hand cradled to his chest. Callahan was on his knees, the rope of Hellebore's weapon in his hand, but he made no move to rise and attempt to use it.

Taiyo had miraculously gotten onto his horse, clutching his still-bleeding side and leaning forward, but he managed to reach her. Emerson fumbled with a pouch on his belt, and Hellebore took that as her cue to go. She clambered up onto the horse behind Taiyo, wrapping her arms around him and taking the reins. She jabbed her heels into the steed's side and took off, leaving them all behind.

She pressed one hand to her husband's injured side, hand staining black all over again.

CHAPTER 26

Hellebore needed to do what she could to stop the bleeding, but with Callahan and Emerson not incapacitated, she couldn't risk stopping until she was certain she'd lost them.

As if he could hear her thoughts, Taiyo pressed his hand over hers, applying pressure to the wound. "I'm alright. I can keep going, sunshine."

"You'd better be," Hellebore said, doing her best to keep her voice level, but it trembled regardless. "You're not allowed to die before you give me an explanation."

"I promise," Taiyo whispered as the trees flew by them while his horse cantered toward Auror.

Eventually, it wasn't up to Hellebore to decide when to stop. Their combined weight, even on Taiyo's strong horse, had the creature huffing and wheezing before noon. Hellebore stopped by a creek, setting the horse to drink while she helped Taiyo down, stumbling when his full weight hit her. She wrapped an arm around him and helped him hobble over to the base of a large tree so he could lean back against it.

She said, "Deep breaths. Give me just a minute. You need stitches."

Taiyo opened his eyes, holding his side. "You don't have a needle."

She ignored him. He was being obtuse because he was delirious from blood loss and exhaustion. Besides, she was still angry at him, even if she chose him.

She stopped by the water first as well, washing the blood off her hands. She dragged her fingers through the creek bank, sandy enough to work for her purposes. Once she'd scrubbed the blood off herself, she returned to the horse, brushing a hand over its flank as it kept drinking from the creek. She ran a hand down its leg until it lifted it for her, displaying the horseshoe on the bottom of its hoof. Hellebore kept one hand wrapped around the ankle, pressing one fingertip on the metal. With her other hand, she drew the formula in the sand and pushed her power into it. She pinched her fingertips together against the horseshoe and turned back around, holding a needle in her hands.

"Clever girl, my alchemist." Taiyo had one eye open and he started chuckling until he coughed up blood and winced. Hellebore made quick work of her other preparations, including tearing up the hem of her nightgown. It was already a lost cause, so she might as well put it to use. Once she had her bandages, a damp clean cloth, and thread through transmutation, she knelt beside Taiyo and started to help him out of his jacket and then his shirt.

He muttered, "If only you were taking my shirt off for better reasons."

"Don't try to be funny. You're lucky I'm willing to help you after everything I heard." Hellebore used the damp cloth to wipe away the blood and grime. "Now be quiet or this will hurt a lot worse."

"You know none of this will matter in two days."

Hellebore slid the needle into his skin and he gritted his teeth, letting out a sharp groan. She focused on stitching the wound closed, but said, "If I don't do this now, there won't be two days to find out."

"Hellebore..." Taiyo breathed in deeply, hissing as he exhaled when the needle went in again. "They burned the garden. There aren't any irises left in Auror. Certainly not enough for you to save me even if we make it back in time."

She didn't need to be reminded.

With no scissors, she leaned in and used her teeth to cut the thread before moving to press her pad of bandages and wrap more around him to secure it. Once she'd tied it off tightly, she looked up at him.

"Maybe I would rather spend these last few hours with you than watch you bleed out."

Taiyo's hand cradled her cheek, skin stained black. Then he kissed her. Hellebore leaned in and returned it, making sure not to aggravate his injury as she wrapped her arm around his other side.

When he pulled back, his lips brushing her cheek as they moved. "I love you. I'm sorry."

Hellebore squeezed her eyes shut as his hands brushed up and down her sides. She pulled her head back just enough to look him in the eyes without leaving his loose embrace. "Why did you lie? Why didn't you tell me? Why did you let me believe my brother thought I was a failure?"

Taiyo closed his eyes and bowed his head. "You know now... I came to your father's court for one purpose, to save my people by taking an alchemist and marrying her so my kingdom's fate would be hers. If I had to pretend like I was going to go to war with Chymes if I didn't get my way, I would. Your father, of course, feared the day I would return after the disastrous end to my engagement to Palladia, so he was quick to agree to my remedy. I didn't pay any attention to whether your brother's silence was real approval or fear. I cannot impress upon you just how desperate I was. And how desperate I was not to let any of them know it."

"If I had refused to help you when you showed me the garden, what would you have done?"

"Presuming all my attempts at reason failed? My worstscase scenario was to lock you in a lab and treat you like a prisoner until you started helping. I didn't want it to come to that, but given I had no idea if I'd be receiving another Palladia as my bride, I had to be prepared for anything. Even if at that point all you did was pretend to work, I had to take the chance I would get a wife who would actually save the irises. I came for you when I had nothing left to lose."

"Keeping Callahan in a cell and then throwing him out of the city?"

Taiyo nodded, fingers curling into the silk. "The last thing I expected to see the morning of our wedding was him. He didn't say it, but of course I suspected he was there, sent by your aunt to take you before I married you. He claimed he only wanted to attend the wedding, but I couldn't take the risk he had something else in mind. Then I showed you the garden and you agreed so quickly to help me... but only because you believed your brother had abandoned you to me. That he thought you weren't a worthy alchemist. Then he started writing. I was terrified your willingness to help, especially when you claimed you would save me too, would vanish if you discovered your brother had not cast you aside. I hadn't hoped—I'd been justifying every awful thing I did, knowing I would pay with my life, but then you were promising to save it. I didn't want to die, and he'd stopped sending the letters by then. So I hid them, even though I hated myself for it. I could see how much it hurt you, and I did it anyway. I can give you all my justifications, but that doesn't change what I did. It doesn't change the fact that I hurt you for my own gain."

Hellebore's voice cracked. "You still never told me."

"I was a coward. I was falling in love with you, and I searched desperately every day for just a hint of affection, and it was never there. How could I bring myself to tell you and seal my fate in your eyes? I promised myself I would tell you if I lived. That I would tell you everything. If I was going to die anyway, I wanted to at least die with the hope maybe in the minutes or hours before you would stop hiding your heart from me."

Hellebore surged forward and kissed him, cupping his jaw in her hands. It wasn't more than a breath, as she pulled back and whispered, "I am furious with you."

"You should be."

"But I told you not to tell me, so I can't blame you for it all."

"I still should have confessed."

"I won't waste this time arguing over it a moment longer." Hellebore let go, pulling out of his arms. She grabbed the horse's reins and led it over to Taiyo. "Daylight is when you are strongest, so we need to keep moving and get back to Auror before the eclipse."

Taiyo sighed, bracing one arm against the tree trunk as he stumbled to his feet. "There's no point, sunshine. There aren't enough irises."

Hellebore shook her head, ignoring the way her eyes welled up at the reminder. "There could still be *something,* so get on the horse. Don't make me repeat myself."

Taiyo complied, and Hellebore vaulted up behind him again, but this time he was at least able to handle the reins, so she could slip her arms loosely around his waist.

"I know you're clever, so you probably already figured it

all out, but since I'm not hiding anything anymore, I should tell you the whole story about what happened twenty-five years ago."

He was right. Hellebore had put together most of it, but she was happy to press her cheek to his back and feel the low rumble of his voice as he filled in the missing details.

King Silas was looking for a way to avoid making Palladia his King's Alchemist, given how notoriously difficult she was and how they never agreed on anything. Then Taiyo arrived, young by elf standards, but Chymes didn't really understand that, or Hellebore's father hadn't cared. Still, he was far too idealistic and naïve, so when Silas had proposed the idea of a marriage alliance, Taiyo had been convinced it was the best way to foster good relations and carry them on into future generations, finally putting to rest the lingering animosity from centuries before.

He'd had no idea Palladia hadn't been as enamored with the idea as he was. Especially since Silas had kept Palladia away from him, claiming it was Chymesian tradition for brides not to interact with their grooms during the engagement period.

"I feel particularly embarrassed I fell for that," Taiyo added.

Taiyo continued, telling her that when they arrived in Auror, Palladia played her part, not affectionate, but not acting as though the arrangement was against her will. She just wanted to be certain she'd be able to continue practicing alchemy, given at the time, it was still outlawed completely. He assured her, but she put on a convincing act —how could she trust him? That was when he showed her the garden of irises, telling her how he would give her one after their wedding, but it wasn't enough. She wanted more. Desperate to keep this engagement and the alliance from failing, as a young king who had yet to prove himself to his court, he was willing to do anything Palladia wanted. Even give her his blood if it meant she would marry him.

He'd never suspected she would use it against him.

When she attacked, she used the blood as a hostage against him, and Taiyo, having no idea of the real limits of alchemy, only the terrible stories he'd grown up with, was willing to give anything to get it back. When he broke the engagement, giving her all the official documentation that she needed to clear her and ensure her brother couldn't use any of it against her, she returned the blood, or so he thought. Taiyo didn't know it at the time, but before she left, she used some of the blood to cause the rot that would slowly eat away at his irises and his kingdom for the next twenty-five years.

That was why he'd tried to cleanse the rot with his blood. His had been used to cause it in the first place.

Hellebore and Taiyo were forced to stop and rest when the sun went down and Taiyo began wheezing with every breath.

They had no food or supplies, so Hellebore transmuted his jacket into a ratty blanket and covered him with it as his eyes fluttered shut. His head was pillowed on her thigh while she leaned against a tree trunk, keeping one eye open and on watch.

She was grateful she had, when halfway through the night the sound of a branch breaking ripped her out of her light doze. Unfortunately, she still had no weapon. She put her hand on Taiyo's shoulder, ready to leap to her feet to protect him if needed when a figure stepped out of the shadows and into the moonlight.

"I'm not here to fight. Or to take you back."

Callahan stood in front of her, arms raised toward his head.

Hellebore gasped when the moonlight struck the glass he held between his fingers. Taiyo's blood.

"What are you doing here?"

"He's dying, isn't he? I'm no alchemist, but I know his blood right now is black and this blood is red. You want to save him, don't you? I thought you might need this."

"Yes, but you don't want me to."

Taiyo wasn't stirring. He was in bad shape. She could feel his heartbeat beneath her fingertips, slower than it had ever been before.

"I didn't realize... You bludgeoned Emerson and sedated our aunt. You were willing to bash my skull in just for the chance to spend a few more hours with him." Callahan held out the vial. "I know you would never have forgiven me if we had succeeded."

Hellebore reached out and took the vial, all without disturbing Taiyo. "I wouldn't have bashed your skull in."

Callahan nodded at the vial. "Can you use that to save him?"

Hellebore looked at it, throat tightening. "Maybe. I don't know. Not without irises."

Callahan ducked his head. "I'm sorry, Hels."

She said nothing, just stared at the healthy red blood.

Her brother took a seat beside her. "You never answered me why."

Hellebore laughed, shaking her head as her vision blurred. "You know why."

"Does he?" Callahan's brown eyes flickered down to Taiyo's face, grimacing in pain even as he slept.

Hellebore curled her fingers around the vial and pressed the cool glass to her heart. "He will."

"I have to go. I'm sure our aunt will have woken up by the time I return and Emerson is a terrible medic. We'll have to get her back to Chymes if we want to save her life, if not her arm." Callahan leaned over and kissed her temple. Then he reached into his bag and passed her a waterskin and a parcel of food. Then he pushed himself to his feet. "Good luck, Hels. I hope he's worthy of it."

"He is, Cal. I promise you, after all of this, you'll see."

"Oh, after all of this is settled, I will make sure of that. If he wants to keep you, he's going to have to deal with me."

Then Callahan was gone, and Hellebore looked back down at the vial.

With this... maybe she didn't need the whole garden. She just needed one.

CHAPTER 27

When dawn broke the next day, Taiyo's words were slurring and his vision was hazy, eyes not quite focusing on her fully. She did her best to get him to eat some of the food Callahan had given her. It hadn't been much, and she was still hungry afterwards, but at least it should get her back to Auror. She looked up at the rising sun. Hopefully Taiyo would improve during the day.

Either way, Hellebore was going to have to ride through the night in order to reach Auror before the eclipse. His horse would just have to deal with it. The beast was already going slower carrying two of them; Hellebore had to make up for it somehow.

She managed to get Taiyo up onto the horse and herself behind him, holding him up against her as they rode. When noon approached, and Taiyo's strength rallied just a hair and she could trust he could hold himself up in the saddle, she slid off and jogged beside the horse for as long as she could.

Her lungs were ready to burst and her legs were

scratched and shredded since her nightgown had been cut to the knees to make bandages.

Every time she started to falter, about to faint from the exertion, sweat pouring down her back, she reached out, pressing her fingers against the saddle back and finding the bump of the vial. Each time it gave her enough strength to take a wretched, gasping breath and keep running.

"Sunshine," Taiyo rasped, leaning forward the fifth time she nearly passed out. "You don't have to do this. It doesn't matter if I'm in Auror or not when the eclipse comes. Just stop and stay with me."

"Don't—break—my—concentration!" Every word came out as a gasping wheeze.

She only made it another two minutes before her legs gave out and she went crashing to the forest floor, Taiyo fumbling to stop his horse before he left her behind. She wheezed a minute before pushing herself off the ground, ignoring the scrapes she'd accrued and climbing up behind him on the horse. She took the reins from him and kicked the horse back into motion, desperately trying to catch her breath.

"I said my goodbyes when I went after you," Taiyo murmured as she wrapped around him, and she knew he could feel her thundering heart and her whole body convulsing where she was pressed up against him, gasping for air. "Haruko knew I wasn't likely to come back. Please, it's alright to stop. You don't have to keep trying. I just wanted to spend this time with you."

"You—are. I'm—right—here," Hellebore huffed, jutting her chin over his shoulder so she could see. "Maybe—this is —how—I—want to—spend—it."

Hellebore kept her eyes peeled as they raced through the forest. No irises.

She stopped only to keep the horse from keeling over

from dehydration. She also took advantage of the water, but they did not rest long. Not even when the sun set and Taiyo could no longer keep his eyes open. His head was leaned back, tucked into her neck, and she thanked every good gene she'd gotten to have a torso tall enough she could see over him.

He bled through his stitches.

She couldn't stop and do anything about it.

Hellebore just focused on keeping Taiyo upright and the horse riding as fast as they could back toward Auror even in the middle of the night. She could feel his sluggish heart fighting with each beat. If she could get him back before the eclipse, if there was even just a single petal left in the garden…

The morning of the eclipse, Hellebore, one arm wrapped around Taiyo, the other steering, raced through the city gates. No one stopped her, thankfully. She didn't know if it was because they recognized Taiyo in her arms or her. Since she looked like a banshee in her tattered shreds, she doubted they recognized her.

When Hellebore brought the horse to a screeching halt at the closed castle gates, a shout went up. "It's the king and queen!"

Soon enough, they were opening and Hellebore brought them through right as Haruko ran out of the palace doors. Haruko's eyes widened when they landed on Hellebore. "You came back?"

"How long until the eclipse?" Hellebore gasped as she moved to dismount.

"Thirty minutes before it begins. Taiyo, is he—"

"Are there any irises left? Any at all in the garden?" Hellebore hit the ground, but her legs buckled and she went to her knees.

"Not that I know of. There might be some in the city

that were cured, but considering how unlikely it is the Moon Elves make it here—"

"Send out whoever you can to go see! And help me—" Hellebore tried to get up from her knees. Her vision was swimming. She needed air. She needed food. She needed water.

She was about to faint.

She reached up and her fingers fumbled with the saddlebag. She dug in and wrapped them around the vial, pulling it out.

She needed to save her husband.

Haruko helped Hellebore to her feet as she held the vial. Haruko looked over her shoulder and barked at the guards gawking at them. "You heard your queen! Get to it! Find us some irises!"

Once Hellebore was on her feet, vision steadying once more, Haruko turned to her and said, "I'll send for healers—"

"Don't bother. If we only have thirty minutes—" Hellebore took a deep breath. "They can't save him. But I can."

She reached up for Taiyo, who was about to topple right off his horse. His side was soaked with blood. His stitches had come undone. Haruko immediately helped her get Taiyo off the horse as he came back to awareness. He caught Hellebore's shoulder and murmured, "Don't leave me."

"I won't. I'm not going anywhere," Hellebore said, taking one side while Haruko took the other. "We're going to go to the garden, can you do that?"

He nodded, eyes tightly shut as he squeezed Hellebore's shoulder. She looked up at the sun. They didn't have long.

If there was just a single petal left...

They went in through the back, Haruko holding open the gap in the branches for them.

Hellebore stumbled into the garden, crashing to her knees with Taiyo and landing in the ash. She called out to Haruko as she came in after them, "Look for a bloom, petals, anything that could still have magic in it!"

Hellebore was careful to leave Taiyo in a comfortable position before she tore through the remains, digging her hands into the ash. It was all black. There was nothing left there.

But there had to be *something.*

Haruko was on the other side of the garden, covered in soot and ash, shaking her head.

Hellebore started to get to her feet, ready to race up to her lab to tear through her notes for a miracle, but then a hand curled into her leg, pulling her back down.

Taiyo was looking up at her. He whispered, "Stop, sunshine, please, just stop."

"The eclipse will happen in a few minutes. I've got to try—"

"I didn't come after you because I thought there was a chance you could save my life. I came after you because I couldn't bear to pass without you being the last thing my eyes see."

Hellebore crashed to the ashy ground beside him, eyes watering. A sob fell out of her throat as he pulled her into his arms. He gently shushed her as he pressed a kiss to her cheek and ran a hand up and down her back, comforting her when he had minutes left of life.

He whispered, "What's all this for then? You don't need to shed any tears for me. You've hidden your heart so well I never stood a chance of finding it. All the better anyway. It means I can't break it as I go to the grave."

Hellebore looked up, mouth opening, but then she spotted a window and a little potted iris sitting in the sunlight. There was still one left in the castle.

Their wedding iris. It was still in her lab.

Hellebore ripped herself out of his arms and took off running despite her husband's protests.

He could thank her when he lived past the eclipse.

She tore through the castle until she reached the lab, grabbing the pot and the belt sitting on the table nearby. She looped it around her waist, depositing the vial of blood in one pouch and filling the others quickly with the equipment she needed for this insane idea.

Once she had it, she tucked the iris into the crook of her arm and raced back to the garden as the sun and moon inched closer together.

Haruko had taken Hellebore's place by Taiyo's side, and as she ran through the ash, she heard him calling her name.

Hellebore came crashing back to his side as the moon passed in front of the sun, and Taiyo opened his eyes. His voice was weak and broken as he spotted her carrying the iris. "Hellebore, please, stop."

"What are you doing? Is one iris enough?" Haruko asked.

She ignored them both as she knelt beside him, reaching into her pouch and pulling out the vial of his blood from before the rot. She grabbed his shirt and ripped it open before pulling out a syringe and a small incision knife.

This definitely wasn't sanitary, but if it would save his life, that's what she would deal with.

Hellebore plucked the bloom of the iris and shoved it into her second syringe, scribbling a quick formula in her notebook with the ash and pushing her power into it, turning the petals into a liquid, brimming with the same kind of magic that was ebbing out of Taiyo, causing the gasping breaths coming from him. She filled the other syringe with his red blood.

As soon as the moon started to creep over the sun, Hellebore injected him with the iris' serum. The iris' magic took effect and his heart kept beating even as his connection to the sun weakened.

Now it was time for Hellebore's real work.

She scribbled a new formula on her arm and started the work of purifying Taiyo's blood. She took the syringe of blood and injected it into his arm. It was a slow process, with only a small fraction of pure blood for her to reference. As she focused on separating the rot from his blood, using the magic of the iris to keep the magic flowing through him, she cut the remaining stitches and used the wound as an exit for her to pull the rot out of him.

Black rot slowly came out, not just blood, and Hellebore breathed a little easier.

She could do this. She could save him.

At least... that's what she thought until she noticed she wasn't purifying his blood faster than the rot was contaminating it again.

And if she stopped, he would die.

"Hellebore! Is it working?"

Haruko clenched the ashy ground as she watched.

Hellebore took a deep breath. "Do you remember what happened when you and your healers tried to give Taiyo a transfusion?"

She'd read about it in his records, Haruko giving almost enough blood that it would kill her in the hopes the healers would be able to give him a transfusion large enough to save him.

"Yes. All it did was spread to the transfused blood. I couldn't give him enough to save him. Our magic is unique to us, my blood with my magic couldn't reverse what had overtaken his."

"Yes, your blood. However, blood without magic would be able to."

"You can't mean yours! You're a completely different species! His body will still reject it."

"Well, it's a good thing I'm an alchemist with control over the chemical makeup and can transmute it into something that his body will accept." Hellebore was already using her free hand to write the formulas.

"But that doesn't solve the problem of it spreading. This could kill you! You could just end up taking on the rot yourself."

"I'm aware. Haruko, reach into my belt, please."

Haruko didn't need to be told twice. She dug through Hellebore's belt, finding the transfusion materials. With a few instructions from Hellebore, Haruko had it ready, slipping the first needle into Taiyo's arm. She turned to Hellebore and asked, "Are you certain? You'll really risk this to save my brother?"

"Yes."

Haruko slipped the second needle into Hellebore's arm. Her red blood filled the first tube. His black blood filled the second. She activated the formulas.

Hellebore pushed her blood into Taiyo as she pulled his corrupted blood into her veins, simultaneously purifying the blood still in him from the rot. She adjusted the chemical makeup of her blood as it entered Taiyo's veins until it resembled his and his clean blood accepted it to replenish his. She also had to keep pulling the separated rot out of Taiyo before it tried to re-corrupt his blood.

It was a miracle she was managing any of this, much less those three crucial things at the same time. But as it was...

It meant she had no ability to do anything about the rot corrupting her blood.

The eclipse took over an hour to reach totality, and when it did, Hellebore still hadn't been able to purge all the rot. She closed her eyes as the world went dark. All that mattered to her was the thrumming sun magic in Taiyo that kept his heart beating and the blood she was cleansing so it would continue to beat.

Taiyo's eyes blinked open as the totality began to pass and the sun and moon began to part. Hellebore's heart started to slow, struggling to keep her blood pumping as she simultaneously poured hers into Taiyo and took his thick, poisonous blood into her, eating away at her life.

"Hell—" He blinked, rasping as more and more of the rot left him, either by being dragged out from the wound on his side or into Hellebore's blood. "Hellebore, what..."

Haruko was at his side, hands on his shoulders, keeping him down. "It's alright, Taiyo. Everything is going to be fine."

"What is she doing?"

Thanks to the transfusion, Hellebore had made excellent progress. Making her blood match the blood from the vial she'd injected in him and using it to replace his corrupted blood was far faster than just cleansing his. She could feel the strength of his magic coming back, filling his blood again as the next hour passed and the sun slowly returned. She gasped as the sun magic in Taiyo's corrupted blood in her began to burn even as it clogged her heart.

"No. No! Haruko, let go—stop her! She's killing herself!"

But it was too late. She'd cleaned the rot from his heart.

By destroying her own.

The needle ripped out of her arm, and her hands fell as red blood began to pour out of the incision on Taiyo's side while black blood poured out of the spot where the needle had been on her arm. She was gasping and choking as her heart began to slow to the tempo of the sluggish beat she had memorized as Taiyo's.

Arms wrapped around her as she was gathered into his lap. Taiyo's face filled her vision while the two celestial bodies parted above them. His hand cupped her cheek and she looked up at him to see tears welling up in his eyes as his voice came out rough and desperate. "Why did you do that? What could ever possess you to do this? How could you do this to me? How could you force me to live after you're gone?"

She reached up and put her hand over his heart, its beat now steady and sure and strong.

She whispered, "There. My heart. It's right there."

His eyes widened but then she slid her other hand to the back of his neck, pulling him down so she could press one last final kiss to his lips. When she pulled back, she could feel blood coming up her throat. "Take good care of it for me."

"No. Don't you dare—"

"Your Highness, we found one!"

Hellebore's eyes rolled in the back of her skull, and her little human heart wasn't strong enough to keep pumping the sludge of her blood a moment longer.

CHAPTER 28

Hellebore woke up to a soft weight on her chest. She blinked and the sunlight cleared for her to see she was in Taiyo's room—really their room, considering how she hadn't slept a night in hers for months.

The weight was a hand resting over her heart. She closed her eyes. Her heartbeat was steady, normal. She was alive.

She opened them again. And her hands... her arms...

They were like tattoos, stretching up from her palm to her elbow, the design of Sunrise Irises across them. A hum settled under her skin.

She couldn't put her finger on it, but she felt... different. Warm, but not the same warm that came from being curled up against a Sun Elf. It was coming from inside.

She knew without looking who the hand on her chest belonged to, and she was correct; her husband was lying beside her, measuring her heartbeat with his palm like she had done so many nights.

His chest was rising and falling. He was alive. She was alive.

Hellebore didn't understand.

Her blood certainly didn't feel like it was black sludge. Her heart wasn't struggling to pump it with every breath.

Taiyo stirred as she sat up straighter. She could see his side was rebandaged, and within a split second, she was engulfed by him again, clutching her to himself before he pulled back and took her face in his hands. "Hellebore, talk to me, how do you feel? Are you alright?"

"Well, I'm not dead, so I feel better than if I was." Hellebore glanced down at her arms before looking back at him. At some point, she'd been changed out of her destroyed nightgown, cleaned up, and put in a new one. She assumed by Phoebe and Elaine. "By the way, how am I not dead?"

His grip on her tightened as his face fell, but he was still ridiculously gentle with her. "I am so furious with you."

Her lips twitched. "Can you be furious with me tomorrow?"

He stared at her for a moment before his lips twitched as well as she grinned at him. "You're alive because I was able to use the iris the guards brought to make a connection with you, the way I did with the irises to try and stop the rot. Thankfully, because you are much smaller than the entire land of Iubar, it worked. I was able to pour enough magic into you to connect my magic to your life. It was enough for me to be able to cleanse without killing myself."

"And these?" Hellebore held her hand up.

"When the healers reached us after the eclipse, they told me it was from the magic now in your blood; the other iris is in mine. That's what connects us."

"Connects us how?" Hellebore furrowed her brow. She'd heard of a ritual connecting an elf and a human, or an elf with human blood like the Star Elves did for their comet, but this didn't seem to be the same thing. "I'm not going to start hearing your thoughts or anything?"

"No, you won't." Taiyo gave her a soft smile. "Our very lives are connected. You have a lengthened lifespan now. We'll go together."

Well, that was unexpected.

"So... I take it that means no second marriage for you?" Hellebore laughed.

"I never wanted one. Since I married you, you are the only wife I want." Taiyo's thumbs brushed over her cheeks, bringing her eyes back up to his. "I'm going to need you to explain yourself to me. Why did you sacrifice yourself to save my life? And don't give me any nonsense about me being your king."

Heat flooded her cheeks and she couldn't stand to look at the intensity in his eyes, but neither did she pull away. "I thought I already did."

"Tell me again."

She dropped her hand to his heart, brushing her fingers over his skin. His heartbeat rose to meet her fingertips like that's what it was made for.

She whispered, "I've never liked why. I always preferred how. But in this case, *where* is the more pertinent question. You always asked me where. Ask me again."

"Where have you hidden your heart?"

She looked up, palm flattening against his heart. "It's right here. You're my heart."

His hands slid to cradle the back of her head.

She shrugged. "I couldn't... I couldn't—" Her voice broke as the image of him lying on the ground, dying came rushing back. "Sorry, I don't—This isn't—I'm not—"

He let out a soft hushing sound as his fingers tangled in her hair. "Sunshine, you know my heart is yours. Tell me plainly, is yours mine?"

She broke, breathing out, "Yes."

Then he was kissing her and she kissed him back. She murmured to him, unable to stop herself, "I love you. I'm sorry. That's why. I love you. And I couldn't do this without you. I didn't want to do it without you. I couldn't bear for you to leave me."

"Don't apologize. Just say it. Again and again, say it until you lose your voice, and when you lose your voice, scream it just by kissing me until there is nothing else, and when you can kiss me no longer and you are too tired to even lift your arms to hold me, I will hold you and listen to your heartbeat and I will hear your heart whisper in every steady beat."

"I will—" Hellebore kissed him again and again as his hands grabbed her waist. "I love you. I don't know how I went so long hiding from it, but no more. Don't let me go."

"Oh, Hellebore, if I was able to let you go, I would have months ago, but I cannot. My alchemist, my wife, my heart... You do not know how long and how often I have dreamed of this."

Hellebore was out of words.

All she could do was prove to her husband how much she loved him with every beat of her full, thriving heart.

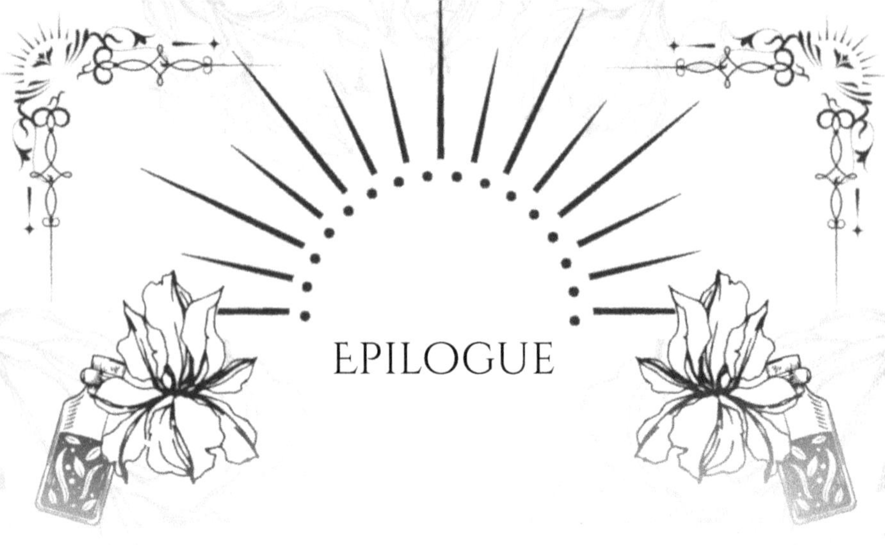

EPILOGUE

The aftermath of the eclipse didn't just include Taiyo's newly recovered health and Hellebore's lengthened lifespan.

In the week following, Taiyo received reports of several Moon Elf attacks that had occurred on the borders. All of them had been wearing plain, nondescript clothes, so they weren't official movements of their military.

But that didn't mean Taiyo didn't swear up and down as he paced their room, ranting about the Moon Elves and their prejudice and belief in their own superiority. He smacked his hand against the reports while telling Hellebore that the Moon Elves they'd caught had to be from the king himself.

Not that Taiyo really wanted it to be an official act from the Moon Elf king, given how much he really didn't want to go to war.

Hellebore did her best to soothe him, reassuring him that the cured irises had allowed them to send the Moon Elves that had started a skirmish running and their king

had easily given Taiyo jurisdiction to do with the ones caught as he saw fit.

Hellebore spent a significant amount of time every day being studied under the guise of checkups by the Sun Elf healers. She kept her complaints in her head, knowing she probably deserved all of it, given her long tenure as an alchemist being the one who usually poked and prodded.

They were all aglow with the thought that the Sunrise Iris and an alchemist who could perform a transfusion could change a human's lifespan so any elf who did fall in love with a human didn't necessarily have to lose them to a human lifespan.

They weren't eager for that to become common knowledge amongst the alchemists, and Hellebore agreed it should be a closely guarded secret. If her aunt had known she could have doubled her lifespan... There were plenty of alchemists who would abuse that information.

Without the desperate need for a cure and finally being dismissed from the healer's purview, her days were shared with Haruko and Taiyo, who began teaching her and letting her take on some of the duties that came with being queen.

It turned out saving her brother's life really did wonders for Haruko warming up to a person.

She kept her lab and was able to run studies and experiments there, but Hellebore was tired of plants, so until something else caught her interest, she was ready for a break from being an alchemist and happy to be a queen.

Taiyo certainly loved the fact that she'd begun actually wearing all the beautiful, elegant Sun Elf dresses he'd had her wardrobe stocked with. He made no secret about it. Hellebore had warmed up quite a bit to the more elegant and less practical clothes, purely for the look in her husband's eyes every time the sun began to set and it painted her in a golden glow.

She'd never cared before about being beautiful, and while Taiyo assured her he loved her in any of her clothes, elvish or alchemist or neither, for the first time in her life, she found herself pulling out nightgowns based on what she thought Taiyo's reaction would be.

She'd never believed marriage could be anything quite like this. Or that she would have a husband who loved her the way Taiyo did.

It was so much better being his wife and not just his alchemist.

Three months after the eclipse, Hellebore rushed out of the castle one afternoon and into the courtyard, ignoring everyone but the brunette climbing off a horse. She didn't stop until she ran right into Callahan's arms as he crushed her to himself.

He laughed. "I told you I'd be coming back."

She pulled back and swatted at his arm. "I didn't expect it to be so soon!"

Callahan shook his head and looked her over. "Hels, what have they done to you? You look like a Sun Elf!"

She reached up and touched her rounded ears. "Don't worry, Cal, it's just a dress."

The door opened behind her, and she turned to see Taiyo following her out after she'd left him in the dust the second Phoebe told her in a stammering voice that her brother was in Auror.

"She looks like the Queen of the Sun Elves, Prince Callahan," Taiyo said, coming down the steps and to Hellebore's side, looping one arm around her waist. Hellebore leaned into his embrace instinctually. Taiyo continued, "We're glad to have you here."

"Oh, don't speak too soon, elf. I'm here to make sure my sister hasn't lost her mind. Don't think you're off the hook with me."

Taiyo extended his hand regardless and smiled. "I look forward to proving myself. As well as showing you my gratitude. I'm told I have you to thank for returning my blood and therein saving my life."

Callahan eyed it for a moment before taking it and shaking it. "You're welcome. And I expect even more gratitude after you hear the news I've brought from Chymes."

They started making their way inside and Callahan looked around and lowered his voice. "Once the healers at the academy declared her stable enough to travel, I escorted our aunt to our father personally. Even if I hadn't, we met up with the guards he sent to bring her in not long after we left the academy. So it wouldn't have been long either way. Her arm was a lost cause by the time the palace healers looked at it, while Father pulled together a trial. It wasn't hard to convince Emerson to throw her under the wagon just by telling the truth. Of course, Father easily forgave me for the role I played and was happy to pin the whole mess on her and charge her with the crime of possessing elf blood as per our treaty. She was found guilty; not even she could talk her way out of it. Sentenced to house arrest at the palace for the rest of her life, stripped of all titles."

Taiyo kept his expression neutral and his gaze ahead as Hellebore's mind whirled, processing everything Callahan said.

"But that's not all of it. She got... rowdy during sentencing and the guards had to step in. Even with a bad arm, she wasn't easy to subdue. When the guards took her down, she started bleeding." Callahan paused, lowering his voice ever further. "Her blood was black."

Hellebore came to a screeching halt, and Taiyo quickly pulled all three of them into the closest room, a random sitting room in the empty guest wing of the palace.

"What do you mean, she bled black blood?" Taiyo hissed.

"Exactly what I said." Callahan raised his hands defensively. "It looked like yours."

"How is that possible?"

Hellebore grabbed Taiyo's sleeve, closing her eyes. "The sedative."

"What?" Callahan asked.

She opened her eyes and let go of Taiyo's sleeve. "I did it. When I transmuted the sedative into her blood the way Emerson did the paralytic into mine, that's what caused it. My hand was covered in Taiyo's blood, so when I grabbed the sedative, some of it got onto the herbs. When I transmuted the sedative, the blood on it went with it. I put the rot in her blood."

Callahan shook his head. "Well, you've stumped every healer in Chymes. They're giving her about ten years before it kills her."

"Sunshine?" Taiyo whispered, hand running up and down her shoulder.

"I'm... I'm alright... I don't... I mean, I didn't mean to, but... I don't want her dead, but what she did to you, Taiyo..." Hellebore closed her eyes and took a deep breath before opening them again. "I don't know what to feel."

Callahan shifted his weight. "What I didn't mention, if this helps, was house arrest wasn't the first sentence she was given. Originally, she was found to be a traitor, and you know how our father deals with traitors."

Hellebore was never going to forget the letter their father had sent outlining what he'd do if she broke the engagement and condemned herself as a traitor.

Execution.

"When she started bleeding black and the healers

investigated it, he changed it to house arrest, since she was going to succumb to the disease eventually. If anything, you gave her a few extra years. Although, I don't know if the two of you think that's worse."

Taiyo murmured, "I wouldn't wish that rot on anyone, even her."

Hellebore remembered how it felt to have the corrupted blood running through her veins even briefly... Taiyo had been living with it for years.

Maybe this was a much better punishment for the crimes she'd gotten away with for years.

Taiyo's fingers laced through hers and he squeezed her hand gently.

"Well, what's done is done. I can't change it now."

Callahan took a seat on one of the chairs, quickly changing the subject. For someone who would one day be king, he wasn't very skilled at handling serious and delicate discussions. "Of course, now the King's Alchemist's position is open, and guess—"

"Emerson, obviously," Hellebore said as she sank into the sofa across from her brother. Taiyo sat next to her, arm draped across the back as she leaned into his side.

If she didn't know how offended he'd be by the suggestion, she'd encourage her brother that he could learn a thing or two about being a king from Taiyo. They still had a lot of ground to cover for Taiyo to win him over.

Callahan gestured at them. "Nauseating. Are the two of you going to be like this the whole time I'm here?"

"Don't act like I didn't catch you with a chambermaid in the east corridor last winter," Hellebore said, and Callahan flushed immediately, pulling at his collar. "Don't complain, my husband and I are hardly worse than that. Need I remind you exactly what I saw with your—"

"That is enough of that from you!" Callahan snapped. "You are still my little sister and I can only stomach so much in one day. Besides, you're exaggerating. It was not that scandalous."

"If it's not that scandalous, why would you be in such a rush to shut me up about it?" Hellebore raised an eyebrow.

Their father had had a conniption when he'd heard of it. While their father was prone to overreacting, it certainly wouldn't have been swept under the rug if the girl had been of a higher status. She'd already warned Taiyo they'd need to keep an eye on Callahan if he started flirting with any girls during his visit.

"I'll have you know there is actually a young lady— actually, no." Callhan cut himself off, cheeks dusting pink as he waved his hand. "You don't need to know anything."

She rolled her eyes and looked up at Taiyo, who was smirking. "He was just about to say whoever is the current object of his affections, he's serious about this time. He says it every time. I'm waiting for him to mean it."

Taiyo laughed, hand shifting up and down her arm.

"Maybe this time I do, but you've lost the privilege of knowing anything about it since you want to run your mouth." Callahan glared at Taiyo's hand on her. "Enough of that too! Seriously, you two are monarchs, why are you looking at each other all doe-eyed?"

"Fine, please, Prince Callahan, enlighten me. What exactly does it mean that your friend Emerson has taken over your aunt's position?" Taiyo asked, shifting slightly to focus his gaze on Callahan.

Hellebore moved just enough so her ear rested on his chest as Callahan launched into telling them of Emerson's misadventures in the last three months.

Taiyo's heart beat strong and steady beneath her. She grinned at what was the beginning of a collection of life she so looked forward to amassing throughout the rest of her days.

For an exclusive behind the scenes looks and bonus content, visit CelesteBaxendell.com and sign up for her newsletter to receive it and more.

WANT MORE ELF ROMANCE?

Enjoyed This Rotting Heart? Want to read about the Star Elves and how King Nyrunn and Idonea were married in order to save their people?

A heartbroken king. A jilted bride. A star-crossed wedding.

Idonea knows the only thing her human blood is good for is its role in strengthening the Star Elves when the comet returns every two hundred and fifty years. Her whole life has been meant for the moment she marries Olaug and finally gets it right, and not even the king can stop her perfect marriage.

The day Idonea was chosen to be part of the Cometa Couple, King Nyrunn was condemned to watching the love of his life spend the rest of hers in the arms of someone else. And he is powerless to stop it.

But when the fateful wedding day arrives, the chosen groom is nowhere to be found. If they don't have a Cometa Couple, the kingdom's magic will weaken and it will be their extinction.

If Nyrunn steps in, he saves his people and marries the love of his life, but what will he do when he discovers he's not the love of hers?

When her husband is the king she fears and despises, will Idonea be able to give him her scarred heart, or will she spend the rest of their lives longing for a husband she never had?

A Note from the Author

Thank you so much for reading *This Rotting Heart!* Taiyo and Hellebore's story was an honor to write, and my privilege to share with you!

I loved getting to share with you all my spin on Hades and Persephone, twisting it just a little so Hades was a Sun Elf and Persephone was the one obsessed with death. I hoped you enjoyed it too!

I'm so excited to continue exploring this world, as I've already written about the Star Elves in *Ties of Starlight*, and I'm so excited to write about the Moon Elves... which will be coming soon, so make sure you're on my newsletter to be the first to hear about it!

If you'd like to help more readers discover *This Rotting Heart,* feel free to leave a review on Amazon, on Goodreads, or on BookBub. I genuinely appreciate every review!

I also want to thank my beta readers, Leigh, Bethany, Caitlin, Jes, Katherine, and Rita, my editor, Carrie, and my proofreader, Myriah. Without them, this book wouldn't have happened!

I hope to see you all again in the next book. Until then, feel free to join me at my website, CelesteBaxendell.com, for behind the scenes content and updates on future books.

254

OTHER BOOKS BY CELESTE BAXENDELL

Rune Heart:

Sacred Heart

Void Heart

Iron Heart

Raven Heart

Shield Heart

Runes of Pain and Peace:

The Prince's Captive

The Prince's Mage

Bewitching Fairy Tales:

Stalks of Gold

Mirrors of Ice

Beasts of Beauty

Cinders of Glass

Songs of Stone

Sands of Deceit

Dreams of Roses

Thorns of Gold

Bewitching Fairy Tales Companion Novels:

Of Chivalry and Revenge

Once Upon A Prince:

The Wicked Prince

ABOUT THE AUTHOR

Celeste Baxendell has always read anything she could get her hands on, but once she read her first fantasy novel, she was hooked and hasn't looked back since.

Her love of magic, adventure, and romance hasn't waned with age, and she endeavors to write nail-biting stories with compelling, complex characters, and finding light in dark times.

She is incredibly blessed to spend her time writing from her favorite chair with her legs curled up under her as she fights the southern heat. When she isn't writing, she's either reading, drawing, or sewing, in that order, and most likely thinking about writing as she does.

For more information about Celeste, her books, or her writing process, go to CelesteBaxendell.com

www.ingramcontent.com/pod-product-compliance
Lightning Source LLC
Chambersburg PA
CBHW051126300726

48981CB00024B/561/J